Beyond Time and Place

28 prize-winning stories written by contestants in Linden Hill Publishing's Children's Story Competition

LINDEN HILL PUBLISHING

Princess Anne, Maryland

www.lindenhill.net

LINDEN HILL PUBLISHING

11923 Somerset Avenue
Princess Anne, MD 21853
www.lindenhill.net

Printed in the United States

Cover art and artwork within book,
unless otherwise stated,
by Jeanne du Nord © 2004.

ISBN 0-9704754-5-4

TABLE OF CONTENTS

Introduction

We set out on this contest with a sense of adventure that is proper for any quest. We did not know who the writers would be, or anything about those writers. Then the stories began to arrive and we were amazed by the variety, the personalities of the writers and their far-off home-places.

The stories were numbered and judged blindly. As the winning stories began to emerge, so too did the tone of the book.

We had stressed in our invitation for submissions that 'children's literature' is a genre, not an age. It is the domain where the thrill of adventure prepares one to face the unpredictable in the every day world and it is that happy realm where possibility can overtake fact.

As we were working on the book, people would ask us about our latest project. They were surprised to learn we were working on a book of children's literature and we were surprised to learn how many adults love to read children's literature when they come home from their busy days of work.

We heard of a person who, once a lover of comic books, now works on Capitol Hill. He has projects due and bills to pay. He now wears ties instead of tees. He said that one day he wandered into a bookstore thinking that he should buy a serious book, maybe a book about politics, economics, or even terrorism.

Then he saw a book about Spiderman, the hero of his youth; 1000 pages of Spiderman comics! That was the book he *had* to buy. Once again, Spider Man saved the day.

That is the stuff of children's literature... the passion, enthusiasm, and exuberance that we ought never to outgrow.

Creativity and genius spring from that state of mind where shapes shift, lines blur, boundaries fade, and the perspectives, horizons, and possibilities are limitless.

In the initial contest guidelines, we asked the writers to create their stories in the traditions of Marc Chagall, Serge Prokofieff, Walt Disney, Escoffier, and on and on through the list of those geniuses who kept their adventurous, curious spirits and their wide-eyed, childlike view of the universe.

There is a wild animal joy that animates all exuberant characters from Snoopy and Winnie the Pooh to Teddy Roosevelt and Albert Einstein.

The title of the book is taken from the ancient initiation ceremony of bards that charges them with recording the human experience and mandates them to 'live beyond time and place.' Also in the ceremony is the line, "You are not alone in your venture; you are accompanied and aided by all those who have gone before you."

While we may stand on the shoulders of giants, it is well known that these creative titans reach their stature by preserving their child within.

FIRST PRIZE

Twilight Among Cheese Clouds
Zander Qlann

Though it may be just hard enough to believe, I promise you the story I'm about to tell almost surely happened one fabulous spring twilight eve.

It had been a glorious day. The sweet, warm smell of lavender and crimson drifted about... dancing... laughing... tickling one's nose at every chance.

The shadows faded to murky purple. The still evening air hushed the robin's newborn chicks.

I climbed into my friendly four-post bed and sank deep into my soft, comfy square-patch spread blanket.

I stared long and hard at my little ceiling... the ceiling stared back without even a word.

The room darkened slowly. The shadows stretched long. The walls and the ceiling seemed to fall down and fade into one.

The coo of a far-off field owl shilly-shallied through the open window. A short, soothing burst of air blew the curtain to the side. The air swirled about for just a moment. The gentle wind bent down and kissed my cheek ever so softly.

I squinted to see the end of the bed. Just then, a curious little pocket mouse, barely one-and-one-half noses tall, scurried into view. He sat himself quite squarely in the middle of my footboard.

Now, it was very obvious this was no ordinary pocket mouse. You see, when he sat, he sat right on his rear with his small hind legs and feet dangling over and under the footboard edge. At the same time, he placed his hand around his chin. The hand held his small head up high. He sat very still, with an everlasting smile, lost deep in his happy thoughts.

"Hello, little friend," I politely offered with a wink.

I surely didn't think he would have anything to say.

"Pleasant twilight eve to you sweet child," my newfound friend snapped back, followed by an unusual small-tilted, silly-thin grin.

I somehow didn't find it strange at all to be talking to this fine-looking little fellow.

"Dear child, I think I'll visit the cheese clouds this eve. I'd be quite honored if you would join me," my new friend politely suggested.

"I would be most happy to accept your kindly offer, other than I don't even know your name, ...nor you mine."

"Forgive me ...I must properly introduce myself. I'm Annatto, Annatto of the Imperial Pocket Mouse Colony. Annatto P. FoxMeyer, the Third, to be exact. You may simply call me Annatto. And yourself, fair lady?"

"I'm Adrianne. My mom calls me Addie. You may call me Addie, too," I quickly answered along with my best Sunday smile.

"Annatto, I'm very excited to perhaps go along with you to visit the cheese clouds this eve. But how on earth will we ever get there?"

"Just leave it to me, Addie."

And with that, he jumped up and ran to the far bedpost. He circled it thrice. His tiny body rubbed close. The post began to glow red, then yellow, then blue, then red again!

In the blink of an instant, six-and-one small balloons appeared. There was a red and an orange balloon, yellow with green, blue then indigo. The last and seventh balloon appeared in a lovely shade of sparkling violet.

In about the same time it takes to give a goodnight kiss to my little dog, Cheddar, a perfect rainbow balloon bouquet floated before my eyes. Glittering gold strings tied fast to the towering bedpost held the balloons firmly in place.

Annatto quickly ran to the other bedpost. The same set of balloons appeared just as the first.

He leapt from the footboard on a run towards

the headboard. Annatto ran headlong across my belly. His tiny feet tickled as he ran. He circled each post just as before. A like set of balloons magically appeared. All four bedposts now had matching sets of rainbow balloons attached tightly to the ends. They bobbed daintily as they tried to break free and float up and away!

"Hang on, here we go, Addie," Annatto yelled.

The whole bed jerked. It tilted to the side a bit and began slowly rising from the floor, upwards.

"Annatto, are we going to run into the ceiling?" I worriedly asked.

He didn't bother to answer. I looked up expecting to run smack into my ceiling with a sudden jolt.

At once, a cool hushed lilac breeze ruffled the bed sheets. Where the ceiling had been, a million-and-one-stars sparkled brilliantly. The silvered crescent speck of the moon twinkled into view. The sun-carved moon danced just a few joyful steps about Orion's corner of the salted springtime sky. I gazed for an endless thought upon a deep, dark periwinkle sky.

We floated gently up…up into the twilight sky. I carefully peered over the side of the bed in search of my house. I only saw far-off multi-shimmering drops of light scattered here and there as if thrown by hands above. There were at least a thousand drops of light as far as my eyes could see.

"Annatto, this is wonderful… floating through the sky. We're lighter-than-air. And I'm in my very own four-post bed. How far to the cheese clouds…will it take long?" I asked as the wind whistled and plucked a pleasant melody amongst the glittering balloon strings.

Once again, Annatto didn't answer.

I carefully explored the fading dusk sky. A shooting star's fleeting shadow gently nudged the wind's soft breeze alongside the dancing balloons.

Annatto stood tall (well, as tall as a nose-and-one-half pocket mouse could possibly stand) atop the center of the footboard walkway. He lifted his little hand cupped over his gleaming eyes. Annatto looked far and wide, searching for any sign of the cheese clouds.

All of a sudden, Annatto pointed skyward while jumping about: "Look yonder, over there, cute girl…there they are! Behold the cheese clouds ahead."

When I looked next, there were clouds everywhere. There were clouds to the left. There were clouds to the front. There were clouds to the right, and then clouds to the rear. The clouds grew bigger and better with each passing minute. There were tall clouds and short. I saw fat ones. I saw skinny. There were clouds with small whirls…even some with tight curls.

One, two, three, then four more, milk-worn edges galore. Puffy squishy fun clouds, crumbly-tumbly cream clouds…clouds cheesy-soft, clouds high aloft, up and down, front and back, side to side, near to far…Clouds!

"I've never been so close to a cloud, Annatto," I very much admitted.

"We will get much closer, and if your luck is

with you, we will even meet a few mayors, maybe a governor, or two. Don't forget their majesties, the King and Queen. Or you may even talk with the President and a few of his Senators. And perhaps...you may even shake hands with the Prime Minister Herself," Annatto declared.

"The Prime Minister Herself!" I exclaimed as I tried to understand.

"Where do they all live?" I curiously asked.

"Each cloud has a cheesekeeper. Each cloud a special flavor. There is the Mayor of Limburger. I once met the Governor of Havarti. Just to name a few. For you see, these are absolutely splendid cheese clouds!" Annatto smugly exclaimed.

"Cheese clouds...you mean to say the clouds are made of cheese?" I asked.

"Why of course. Don't be silly. Why else would one call them cheese clouds?" Annatto neatly answered my question with another.

"Look starboard, fair maiden. Behold a yellowed-ivory Swiss cloud."

The cloud had holes upon holes. Small holes, black holes, mediums and big...holes everywhere!

"A sure favorite indeed," Annatto added.

At that, we swayed near. Annatto jumped from my bed to the cloud. He quickly vanished down one of the many medium black holes. As fast as Annatto disappeared, he reappeared with two other mice. They were elegantly dressed in long, fuzzy green and purple robes with arched-tipped brown leather shoes. They wore dazzling, brightly spangled jeweled crowns atop their jiffy heads.

"Allow me to introduce the King and Queen of

Cherry Stone Swiss," Annatto officially announced.

"If you please, may I present my new best friend, Addie, and her lighter-than-air four-post balloon bed," Annatto stated as he pointed his entire arm towards me with a polite bow.

"Pleased ta–taa–TO meet you... your majesties," I stammered back.

With that, Annatto jumped back to the bed, nibbling a delightful slice of Cherry Stone cheese. We fancied a thanks and a noble goodbye to their majesties, the King and Queen of Cherry Stone Swiss.

"Quickly, we must move about. Onward to other grand cheese clouds, Addie."

Around the next twist, by two or five windfalls to port, a very large, yet somewhat crumbly looking cloud, floated 'cross our bow.

"What kind of cheese cloud could this possibly be, Annatto?"

"I'm almost sure it's Ricotta... Ah yes, look... there's Senator Ricotta without a doubt."

I could see a rather large dormouse atop the cheese cloud. He was sharply dressed in coattail jacket with wire-rim spectacles. He had a matching white top hat and a squiggly, polished wood walking cane. Senator Ricotta waved excitedly about.

"Welcome to my humble cheese cloud, my friends," the Senator called out.

He threw Annatto a lovely chunk of cheese from the cloud.

Annatto handed me a small piece for a taste. It

was quite delicious. The chunk practically melted as soon as it touched the tip of my tongue.

We bid a quick thanks and farewell to the Senator as we lazily drifted on by.

"Look far, not beyond... it's President Parmesan," Annatto shouted as he pointed with one hand and waved with the other.

The President was a short, stout mouse. He was fully clad in jet-black tuxedo with white French-cuffed shirt. He smartly wore a black and white polka dot bow tie with matched white winged-tip shoes. All tooth and smile, he waved back from the triangle shaped cloud as if we were best friends.

As we passed by, the President tossed us a smidgen of cheese, just as the other cheesekeepers had. We thanked him much the same.

The bed coasted on, 'tween a mist and twelve twinkles. The clouds drifted by, amid apple sweet sprinkles.

Bright flashes far away, with a rumble or two, as some melting cheese storm clouds moved out of our view.

The cheese clouds now hung low in the sky. Gold and white candy cane moonbeams danced wildly about the landscape far below.

Annatto looked quickly, with a frown. His nose and whiskers carelessly twitched about his handsome face. By now, I was sure something was wrong.

"I believe this next cloud belongs to Prime Minister Gorgonzola Herself, a very important mouse indeed!"

And at that moment, a tall, bright, and beautiful mouse appeared high atop the cheese cloud. She stood still as a carved stone statue. She wore a simple, charming sharp-pressed full-length golden silk gown. At least twenty-one platinum, silver and gold medals dangled from flowing white ribbons around her neck.

In the Prime Minister's hand, she held a yellow chiffon umbrella against her shoulder. The umbrella canopy balanced gracefully over her head. At the tip of each umbrella rib hung a single glistening yellow puffball. I counted eight in all. The puffballs danced merrily about in the wind.

"The Prime Minister Herself has never parted with a piece of her cheese cloud for a common colonial pocket mouse such as me," Annatto whispered in my ear.

"Well, we'll just have to ask her Excellency to make an exception this time," I boldly proclaimed.

"Prime Minister Gorgonzola Herself, could you perhaps please spare a small nibble of your charming cheesy cheese cloud?" I politely asked.

"Of course young lady, my finest piece for you and your good friend," the Prime Minister (Herself) answered right back.

She cast two portions of Gorgonzola our way.

Annatto smiled broadly as he licked his lips and said, "Thank you... thank you so much your Excellency, I now know... a kindhearted lady indeed!"

We said our good-byes as we slipped up with a slight sway. I now noticed we were drifting farther and away.

The cheese clouds grew small as we floated into the clear, fresh twilight dusk air.

Heavy head 'gainst my pillow, Annatto beside, with eyelids marching down my now weary blue eyes. I breathed in the bittersweet aroma of crisp, hot-from-the-oven milky-marshmallow cheese pies.

"Good late evening Mayor Limburger. And good late night Governor Havarti," I stated aloud. A great wide yawn spread from one ear to the other.

I continued to speak slowly, as if in my dreams. "Good morrow to their majesties: the King and Queen of Cherry Stone Swiss. Good dusk and good speed to you Senator Ricotta and President Parmesan. Especially a fond good twilight eve to you...Prime Minister Gorgonzola Herself."

The bed seemed to settle lightly with a slight, snugful, small shudder.

"Goodnight Annatto. Sleep well," I muttered, a wee bit sleepishly.

I barely remember hearing Annatto respond: "Goodnight sweet Addie, my precious friend. Until the next warmhearted spring twilight eve...as we float gently among cheese clouds yet once upon again!"

ZANDER QLANN BIO

Minutes from being born on the Staten Island Ferry, Zander Qlann held out long enough to be born on tiny Governors Island, one ferry stop from the Statue of Liberty. The world has been his island ever since.

Zander grew up in Washington D.C.; Albuquerque, New Mexico; San Antonio, Texas; Denver, Colorado and Sierra Vista, Arizona. An Air Force pilot's career followed with numerous nights spent soaring over vast oceans and countless days logged exploring far-off cultures and continents. Between adventures, he stopped long enough to earn his undergraduate degree from the University of Arizona and a Master of Aeronautical Science from Embry-Riddle University.

When he takes time from his burgeoning writing career, Zander can currently be found piloting aircraft for a major U.S. airline. He spends his days off on the Chesapeake Bay in Edgewater, Maryland. Zander Qlann's family includes his son, stepson, and one precious little daddy's girl.

SECOND PRIZE

B.J. And The Babe
Sandy Sheppard

What a way to spend a Saturday, eleven-year-old B.J. thought as he followed his mother down the hall of the nursing home. He waited as she peeked into a half-closed door and then pushed it open.

"Hi, Grandma," she said cheerfully. She pulled B.J. into the room.

"Hello, Diane. Who's this you've brought with you?" His great-grandmother's voice sounded weak but her eyes twinkled.

B.J. felt guilty for arguing with his mother

19

about coming. He really did love G-G, but all his friends were playing baseball at the park. G-G reached out a thin hand and ruffled B.J.'s red hair. "So you wore your Yankees shirt!"

B.J. smiled. "This is my favorite t-shirt." He sat down next to his great-grandmother's bed and tossed a baseball from hand to hand.

G-G introduced them to the woman in the other bed. "Lucille, this is my granddaughter Diane, and B.J., her son. Lucille Jefferson is my roommate."

B.J. turned around and found Mrs. Jefferson staring at him. "Come talk to me, Wesley," she said.

B.J., confused, looked at his great-grandma. "Lucille sometimes gets a little mixed up," she told him. "Her son's name is Wesley."

Mrs. Jefferson thought she saw a ball in B.J.'s hand. "Take good care of that ball," she advised. "Not many boys have Babe Ruth's signature on a ball."

B.J.'s eyes opened wide.

She went on, "I remember the day your dad took you to the game between the Yankees and the Red Sox. You hung around the Yankees dugout after the game until Babe Ruth came out and signed your ball. You got an awful sunburn. Redheads have to be so careful."

B.J. could hardly believe it. Mrs. Jefferson's son had a ball signed by the Babe! He wanted to hear more, but Mrs. Jefferson closed her eyes.

"Lucille sleeps a lot," G-G said quietly. "She had a stroke."

20

B.J. and his mom stayed awhile longer; then Diane stood up. "Well, Grandma, B.J. and I had better be going. We don't want to wear you out."

B.J. hugged his great-grandmother. "See ya soon, G-G."

In the car on the way home, B.J. bounced up and down. "Mom, can you drive by the park so I can see if the guys are there? Boy, do I have a story to tell them!"

B.J. grabbed his baseball glove and jumped out of the car. His friends were still playing, so he ran to his usual position in left field.

After the game, the guys gathered around him. "Where were you, Beej? We might've won if you'd been here!"

"I had to go see my great-grandma. She's in a nursing home."

Josh snorted. "Aw, man. You couldn't drag me into one of those places."

"Listen, guys. There was this other lady in the room. She was old, and I mean *old*. She thought I was her son Wesley...."

The boys whooped with laughter. "Is she nuts or something?"

B.J. grinned. "Nah. She's just forgetful. She talked about the time Wesley saw a Yankees game. Wesley got the Babe to sign a ball for him!"

Craig whistled. "Are you kidding? The Babe? Wow!"

The next Saturday B.J. visited G-G again with his mother. He walked into G-G's room first, but before he could say "Hello," Mrs. Jefferson saw him. Her face lit up.

"Wesley, you're back. Come sit by me."

B.J. looked at his great-grandmother. She smiled and nodded.

He felt funny about being called Wesley, but he pulled a chair up to Mrs. Jefferson's bed. She took his hand and patted it. "Looks like the Yankees are going to beat the Cubs in the World Series."

B.J. didn't know what to say, because the baseball season had hardly begun. School had just let out for the summer. "I sure hope so," he answered. The Yankees are my favorite."

"They've won the first three games. Babe Ruth hit a home run after some Chicago fans threw tomatoes at him. Guess he showed them!"

"Yeah," B.J. agreed.

"I'm tired," Mrs. Jefferson said. She closed her eyes, and B.J. turned his chair the other way.

"You're a good boy to talk to Lucille," G-G said. "I told her son Wesley about you."

"You mean Wesley comes here?" B.J. looked surprised.

"He comes every week. I showed him your picture, and he said you look a little bit like he did at your age."

B.J. scratched a mosquito bite on his knee. "I feel funny when she calls me Wesley."

"I know." G-G smiled. "Now, tell me about your plans for summer vacation!"

Every Saturday, B.J. and his mother visited the hospital. Some days Mrs. Jefferson seemed all right, and other days she called him "Wesley."

22

B.J. didn't mind going, as long as he was able to play baseball with his friends afterward.

One Saturday B.J.'s mother was behind schedule. "I guess you'll have to miss your game today. I'm sorry, but your visits mean so much to Grandma," she told him. "And Mrs. Jefferson," she added.

"Aw, Mom!" B.J. smacked his catcher's mitt on the table.

"You play almost every day, and you know I can only visit the nursing home on weekends."

"Come on, Mom. G-G won't mind." But B.J. knew that wasn't true. G-G *would* miss him.

"No more arguments. You're going with me," his mother said firmly. B.J. knew begging would get him nowhere except into trouble. He stormed out of the kitchen and slammed the door.

Staring out the window all the way to the nursing home, he hoped Mrs. Jefferson wouldn't be confused today. It was weird when she held his hand and talked to him about things in the past. His friends were even starting to call him "Wesley."

As B.J. reached the door to G-G's room, it opened and a gray-haired man stepped out. The man studied him for a minute. "You must be B.J.," he said. "I've heard about you. I'm Wesley Jefferson."

B.J. stared at him. *You're old*, B.J. thought. *Your hair isn't even red any more!*

B.J.'s mother shook hands with Mr. Jefferson and then went inside to talk to her grandmother. B.J. stayed in the hall.

"Your mom told me all about the 1932 World Series," B.J. said.

Mr. Jefferson laughed. "I'm not surprised! We heard it on the radio. The Yankees won four straight and took the series. I was about your age."

"Do you still have the ball that Babe Ruth signed?"

"Sure do." Then he remembered something. "I've been carrying this around in case I met you some day." He pulled a picture out of his wallet. "That's me in fifth grade, third from the left in the back row. I can see why my mother calls you Wesley. My hair was the same color as yours. I had freckles too."

B.J. studied the picture but couldn't tell if he looked like Mr. Jefferson. The picture was in black and white. He handed it back.

"I'd better let you visit your great-grandmother. Thanks for being kind to my mother."

B.J. stared at the floor. "That's ok. She's a nice lady." He looked up with a grin. "And she sure knows baseball!"

"She sure does!" Mr. Jefferson agreed. "It was nice meeting you, B.J. Maybe I'll see you again."

"Bye." B.J. waved as he stepped into G-G's room. He glanced at Mrs. Jefferson but she was sleeping.

The next Saturday B.J. was ready before his mother called him. He had read a book about Babe Ruth, and he had some questions to ask Mrs. Jefferson.

He pushed open G-G's door. Mrs. Jefferson's

bed was neatly made. "Hi, G-G. Where's Mrs. Jefferson today?"

G-G's eyes filled with tears. "I'm sorry, B.J., but Lucille Jefferson died this morning."

B.J. swallowed hard. He didn't know what to say.

His mother squeezed his shoulder. He sat down with his back to Mrs. Jefferson's bed. He didn't want to look at it. It was too empty.

*****

Nearly two weeks later the doorbell rang after dinner, and B.J. opened the door.

"Mr. Jefferson! How did you know where I live?"

"Your great-grandmother told me. B.J., I have a present for you." He held out an old shoebox. "You'll understand when you open it."

"Thanks, Mr. Jefferson," B.J. said, surprised. "I didn't expect a present." He paused. "I miss your mom," he said softly.

Mr. Jefferson looked down at B.J. "I miss her too." He turned toward his car.

B.J. closed the door and carried the shoebox into the kitchen. Inside, wrapped in tissue paper, was a scuffed and worn baseball. B.J. picked it up carefully and turned it over. He gasped. "Mom! This is the ball that Babe Ruth signed!"

The box also held a note. B.J. pulled it out and read:

Dear B.J.,

Your visits meant so much to my mother. Thank you for being her friend. I never had a child of my own, but I always hoped I'd find a boy who would appreciate my baseball signed by Babe Ruth. My mother found you for me! She would agree that the ball should be yours.

Wesley Jefferson

B. J. looked at the ball in his hand. He ran his fingers over the name signed in dark blue ink over sixty years ago. "Thanks, Mrs. Jefferson," he whispered. "I'll never forget you."

SANDY SHEPPARD BIO

Sandy Sheppard has been published in over sixty magazines and is the author of one children's book, AVARICIOUS AARDVARKS AND OTHER ALPHABET TONGUE TWISTERS. She has worked as a second grade teacher, accounting clerk, title insurance policy typist, and employment counselor.

Currently she is a freelance writer and substitute teacher. "B.J. and the Babe" is her first short story. It won awards in several competitions but had never been published, and Sandy is delighted that children will finally have a chance to read it!

She lives in Vassar, Michigan with her family and a cockatiel, a hamster, a cat, an aquarium with numerous fish, hundreds of stuffed animals and Beanie Babies, and many shelves full of children's books.

THIRD PRIZE

Jeremy
Thomas Lynn

Jeremy Prentiss, a recent arrival at the Gate, hoped to return as a cat. Imagine his disappointment to learn that only dogs were available.

"Nobody wants to be a dog," he muttered to no one in particular.

"You may be right but only dogs are going back right now," a voice said.

Startled, Jeremy looked around and saw a man sitting in front of a huge golden book in which he evidently had been writing. The man had an imposing countenance and a long white beard. He set his pen down and was instantly attentive.

"Excuse me," Jeremy addressed him. "What did you say?"

"I said that only dogs are going back at the moment."

"Who are you?"

"I am the angel of reincarnation," was the reply. "My name is Hextholdjub, but everybody just calls me Heck."

Jeremy assessed the situation. "Well, Heck. I really wanted to be a cat."

"I am sorry, but there's a long waiting list for cats, so if you want to go back anytime soon, I suggest it be as a dog." The angel seemed truly apologetic. "You can see for yourself," he pointed at his Registry book. "If I go back as a dog, would it have to be one of those small yapping canines?"

"Goodness sakes, no," said Heck. "You can be a beautiful Collie, a Doberman or any other dog of your choice."

Jeremy, being an old-fashioned guy, always considered part of the attraction of dying to be the happy reincarnation as a fawn-colored Abyssinian. Needless to say, he was a feline admirer. Now, he was being asked to return as a... mutt! What did he know about dogs anyway? Except for pulling sleds and toting brandy snifters around their necks, what did dogs do besides howl and chase cats. A dog was a cat's mortal foe. How could Heck possibly expect him to join the enemy camp? He wondered how long he would have to wait to be reincarnated as a cat.

"That's kind of hard to say," Heck mused. "It might be a very long time before your turn comes back around. The last cat departed exactly twenty-seven minutes ago. But there are still plenty of dogs to choose from."

"Well heck, Heck. There seems to be no other option. I have to return as a dog if I'm going back anytime soon."

"That's the way I see it."

So Jeremy studied pictographs of various dogs awaiting embodiment. St. Bernards, Mastiffs, and Great Danes were promptly rejected. He was certain they required much more food and he didn't want to spend his time filling his belly. It was difficult to make his selection, but he finally decided on a Dalmatian as the least objectionable.

*****

Mary Frances wanted a puppy for her birthday. Father promised, and that was her wish as she blew out the candles on her cake. The family gathered around to sing "Happy Birthday" and to watch as she opened her gifts. She couldn't help feeling a little sad because she didn't see a puppy anywhere.

Then her father told her, "You have one more present to open." She squealed in delight as she saw for the first time the little round ball of fur with big brown eyes and a red ribbon around its neck.

"Oh daddy!" she cried as she mothered it with hugs and kisses. "It's just what I wanted and I'm going to call him… Jeremy."

Jeremy was as contented as Mary Frances when she carried him all around the house and showed him off to her friends. In the evening, she mixed some chewy puppy chow with warm milk and set it beside his water bowl. He waded through the water to get to his dinner and she laughed at his antics.

"You'll soon learn," she told him.

It was a large house and her bedroom was up-stairs. That's where she also made his bed. Jeremy was happy that he would be sleeping near the little girl whom he was beginning to like very much. He was dismayed, however, when she placed him inside a cardboard box beside the bed. Suppose he needed to go to the bathroom. How was he expected to get out of that box?

Incidentally, he thought, *exactly where was he expected to go to the bathroom?* He looked around but saw only a small pillow and some newspaper in a far corner. *Oh, No! ... Surely not in the same box!* He shuddered at the idea. *At least a cat would have some sand.*

He had spent a hectic time since his birth, or rather his rebirth. The first few weeks were vague in his memory and he could barely recall parting from his siblings of various colorations and from his mother, who was beautiful with black spots on her white coat. It was peculiar learning how to walk with four legs instead of the customary two. Even now, he was slightly uncoordinated and fre-quently tripped when he forgot to move his two front feet. He would have been more graceful as a cat.

It was bedtime but he wasn't at all sleepy. He wanted out of the box so he could explore his new surrounding. "Hey little girl," he called out. "Mary Frances, Mary Frances, wake up!" But it was her father who heard the noise and came into the room.

"Honey," he shook his daughter awake. "Jeremy is whining because he's lonely."

She rubbed her eyes. "I know daddy, but what can I do?"

He handed her a large alarm clock. "Put this in the box with him and maybe its ticking will settle him down."

Jeremy was puzzled when she placed the clock beside him. *I don't need to know what time it is*, he complained. *I'm not going anywhere.* He continued to fuss. Finally, the girl picked him up and set him near her pillow.

"Now you won't be lonesome anymore," she said. Jeremy was glad to be out of the box and he showed his gratitude by licking her face until they both fell asleep snuggled against each other.

The next day began Jeremy's education. He was still wobbly on his feet but quickly mastered the art of descending the stairs. The girl was a big help as she taught him to take each step one at a time, head first. Going down the stairs was quicker than going up because once or twice he missed his footing and rolled completely past a step. Jeremy would have to grow some before he would be able to stand on his hind legs and reach a higher step.

"He's a very smart puppy," her father said. "It must be a frightening experience to point your head down the stairs for the first time and move downward like that."

It's not such a big deal, Jeremy remarked to himself.

The rest of the morning was a circus for both girl and puppy. They chased each other, rolling and tumbling until mother brought them to a halt for lunch and a nap. Jeremy was thirsty and his legs were very tired. He found his water dish and avoided stepping in it this time as he lapped it dry. Upstairs in the bedroom, Mary Frances again put him in the cardboard box for his nap.

"I'm sorry Jeremy, but daddy says you have to get used to sleeping here." Then she put a small hand mirror in the box with him. She hoped he would see his reflection and not be so lonesome.

He objected mildly because he wanted to lie once more on that big soft pillow, and then he saw himself in the mirror. *Wait a minute,* he thought. *Is that me? I'm supposed to have black spots and a white coat like my Dalmatian mother. Where are my black spots?* He inspected his image closely but all he could see was brown hair everywhere he looked. There were no black spots anywhere. "There's something wrong here. Hey! Little girl, something's not right."

Mother heard the racket and came upstairs to see what was the matter. "Why is the puppy barking so loudly?"

Mary Frances laughed and said, "He sees himself in the mirror and thinks there's another dog in there with him." They both watched as Jeremy first gazed at the mirror and then up at them with a quizzical expression.

Jeremy realized they were unaware that he was supposed to be a Dalmatian so he quieted and looked at himself in the mirror. He saw a small shorthaired dog with big brown eyes and floppy ears gazing back at him, and then he saw his short stubby legs ... extremely short and extremely stubby! By no stretch of the imagination did he resemble a Dalmatian. It looked more like, he searched his memory, like a ... a basset hound! *Oh my Gosh, I'm a pipsqueak of a basset hound!* He then did what bassets do best; he howled. He howled until Mary Frances was forced to cradle him in her arms and let him lie on her big soft pillow. She petted and stroked him and he finally slept and dreamed of being a purebred Abyssinian.

Jeremy eventually accepted his situation and no longer felt sorry for himself. He had the run of the house and also explored the far reaches of his fenced back yard while Mary Frances was at school. However, it was the front yard that held the greater fascination, but he was not allowed there.

His favorite spot was near the fence gate where the sun bathed him with warmth and the birds serenaded from the limbs of stately oak trees. From there he observed the world parading before him. School buses passed with chattering boys and girls and he greeted the postman and delivery people as they made their scheduled visits. Twice a week he could bark at the trash men and once in a while a stray dog, usually a very large one, wandered by on its way toward adventure. The main attraction from his vantage point, however, was the house directly across the street. It was in that house where a majestic, very graceful, snow white Manx, lived.

Some day, he thought, *I will meet that cat.*

Jeremy enjoyed chasing the few squirrels that ventured into his back yard but they surely had no fear of being caught by his short stumpy legs. They seemed to taunt him in their bold approach and he could only watch with envy as they quickly scrambled up a tree trunk to elude him. He always returned to his place near the fence gate to await Mary Frances from school and to possibly glimpse the white Manx. He still slept next to her bed at night but he now had a wicker doggie bed instead of the cardboard box. Sometimes when mother wasn't looking, he sneaked onto the bed to stretch out on the big soft pillow.

One day he discovered the earth near his fence to be quite soft. He was soon able to dig enough dirt away to squeeze through and he found himself in the front yard! Keeping close to the bushes at the side of the house, he ran around to the front porch. Suddenly, he dropped low to the ground for there, before his eyes, was the snow-white Manx!

It was pure white, not a hair of another color could be seen, and it was tailless, a magnificent show cat. Jeremy's heart leaped and he would gladly have changed places with that cat. The least he could do was walk over and be friendly. *Lord knows,* he thought, *I could use a friend to talk to around here.*

He trotted up to the curb and stopped to look both ways. *Some habits never die.* Seeing the road was clear, he bounded across the street. However, when he approached the cat, he saw the hair rise on its back and he heard "Ssst!" The Manx was alarmed by Jeremy's approach.

"Hey, it's all right. I'm a friend."

The cat retreated but lashed out with an unsheathed claw, missing Jeremy by a whisker.

"You stupid cat! You almost scratched me."

The Manx bared its teeth and continued to hiss.

"What's wrong with you? I don't want to fight. Again, the cat struck at him with its claws. Jeremy ducked. "Well, you're not the kind of friend I had in mind."

"Ssst! Ssst!"

"Shut up, you dumb old cat."

The cat stopped its backward motion and began a slow circle but Jeremy wanted no part of those sharp teeth and claws. He backed away and then he heard someone calling his name. It was Mary Frances and he saw her running toward him from across the street.

"Jeremy," she called out to him. She failed to stop at the curb and was running directly into the path of an oncoming truck.

"Stop! Mary Frances. Stop!" Jeremy tried to shout but the girl heard only excited barking. He ran toward her to halt her headlong rush into the street but he was too late. Brakes squealed as the truck driver swerved and brought his vehicle to a stop.

Mary Frances lay sprawled on the pavement. Jeremy had hurled himself at her and knocked her safely away. It was his small body that was hit by the truck and now he too lay in the street... but he would not rise.

*****

Everything was bright and dazzling and Jeremy recalled his previous visit to this place. The marbled halls were the same. There was the huge Registry book, and the angel Heck writing more entries. "I see this is your second time around," he said.

"You don't remember me, do you?" Jeremy asked. "I wanted to return as a cat..."

"Yes, I remember you now." The angel was genuinely sad, "I am sorry it didn't work out for you."

"Oh, but it did!"

"You mean, you didn't mind going back as a dog after all?"

"I was disappointed at first but I met this little girl, you see, and then I met a cat."

"Ah! I do see," said Heck. "I apologize for the mix up with the Dalmatian, I really do. However, I now have the prettiest tabby for you. He's a shorthaired Abyssinian with a fawn-colored coat lightly ticked. I immediately thought of you."

"Well, Heck. Actually, I was hoping you might have another little basset hound."

"As a matter of fact," the angel interrupted, "I do and I know a little girl whose father promised her another basset hound with short stumpy legs, just like the one she recently lost."

If Jeremy, the human, had been the possessor of a canine tail, it would have been wagging at that moment. However, Jeremy, the basset, did have a tail and it was indeed wagging with joy.

THOMAS LYNN BIO

Thomas Edward Lynn is a former columnist for Sharing & Caring Magazine and his bylines have appeared in various fiction publications. He is also the author of "Old Comrades" a poem carved in granite as a memorial to Korean War veterans at the Mount Hope Cemetery in Bangor, Maine. He currently resides in Lawrenceville, Georgia.

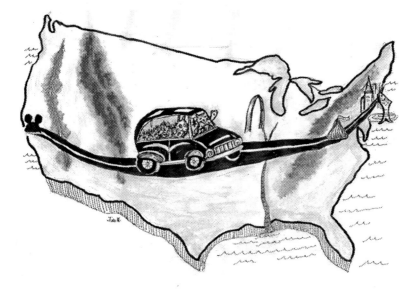

Tuck's Tales, California To Connecticut
Debbie Steltz

Meet Callie, a calico cat, who lives in a cottage on the coast of California.Callie was always a curious cat. One day Callie had a crazy idea. She wanted to visit her good friend Candy, the catfish, who lived in Connecticut. So, Callie called her good friend Carlos, the caterpillar, who lived around the corner, to come along. Carlos, a courageous caterpillar, was very excited to go. YES, YES, YES he shouted with joy!

Callie and Carlos packed their suitcases, cameras, camcorders, snacks, and a map. And off they went in their car across the country. Before leaving California, Callie and Carlos stopped at a huge carnival called "Disneyland." They rode the carousel, ate cotton candy, caramel apples, and corndogs, and drank cold ice drinks.

As they left California, they crossed into the next state, Nevada. In Nevada, they saw a huge concrete wall called the "Hoover Dam." In Utah, there were many snow-covered mountains. Callie and Carlos put on their coats and caps and took a cable car to cross the mountains. It was sooooo cold at the top of the mountains. They followed the Colorado River, which took them into Colorado. To cross the river, Callie and Carlos took a canoe and rowed with carved sticks called oars.

Callie and Carlos were getting very tired. When they got to Kansas, they camped with their good friend Colve the coyote, and Cipper and Capper the cricket twins. They told campfire stories and drank lots of hot cocoa! The next morning, they had a big breakfast before leaving again on their trip. They had cantaloupe, crumpets, and big glasses of milk.

As they left Kansas, they drove into Missouri. Here they saw a huge "C" called the Arch. In Illinois, they traveled through Chicago, called the windy city. In Ohio, they were ready for some fun. They went to the Cincinnati Zoo. They saw crocodiles, camels, big cats, chimpanzees, caribou, creepy lizards, and crawly snakes.

In Pennsylvania, they drove through the city of Chocolate, called Hershey. They strolled down Cocoa Avenue, where the streets are like chocolate rivers and the streetlights are shaped like candy kisses. In New York, Callie and Carlos took a taxicab. They saw Central Park, a big park with birds and concerts. They saw many skyscrapers that are high as the clouds, including the Chrysler building, a building for a carmaker.

Finally, they could see a sign. WELCOME TO CONNECTICUT. They knew they were here!!!

Carlos and Callie drove to Candy's Country Café. Candy was a cook at the café. Candy was so happy to see her friends. She knew they must be hungry, so she gave them her favorite menu. Wow – look at all the choices!!

Breakfast:
Crepes and Cantaloupes
Crunchy Cornflakes
Lunch:
Codfish
Cooked cauliflower
Caramel Carrots
Croissants

Dinner:
Cabbage Rolls
Creamed Corn
Cool Cucumbers
Cornbread

Desserts:
Chocolate Cake
Coconut Cookies
Ice Cream Cones

Drinks:
Crème Soda
Cola Drinks
Cranberry Cocktail

That night, Candy took Callie and Carlos to a concert. They saw children in costumes, heard clarinets and coronets playing, and choirs singing. After the concert, everyone went back to Candy's cabin. As Callie and Carlos snuggled all cozy in their cots, they closed their tired eyes. Their faces smiled, as they remembered their big trip across the country – from California to Connecticut.

DEBBIE STELTZ BIO

Debbie Steltz was born in Milbank, a small town in Northeast South Dakota. She was the oldest of three girls. As a child, she was ornery, full of energy, adventurous and an animal lover. Debbie moved to Kansas after High School and pursued careers in the medical field. Opportunities ranged from nursing to technology.

It was with the reading of numerous children's books to her son Tucker that motivated her to create her first book of Tuck's Tales, California to Connecticut. The book is intended to teach the young reader about the United States in an entertaining manner. It is hoped that adult readers will appreciate the method of teaching children through words and fantasy.

There's An Alien On The Internet
Joanne Peterson

Joey's my best friend. I met him on the Internet. At school recess I play Star Wars with Kevin and Rob, but it's all the neat stuff I learn about the solar system from Joey that makes our Star Wars games fun. Joey doesn't go to school. He's home schooled. I wish Joey went to our school, then I'd never get bored 'cause he's so smart.

Last week my teacher, Mrs. Becker, put a big circle on the blackboard and said it was a pizza pie. "Andy," she said to me, "If I were to divide the pizza, would you like one-third or one-tenth?"

Ten is a bigger number, so that's what I picked. Kevin started waving his hand in the air shouting that he chose one-third. Mrs. Becker drew lines on the circle showing his piece of the pie was bigger than mine.

"Andy's gonna get hungry," Kevin teased. Sandra, who sits behind me, started to snicker. Then the whole class was laughing. I wished the recess bell would ring, and started planning how I would take out a basketball and play by myself at recess, when Mrs. Becker's stern voice quieted the room.

"Andy, do you see how the more you divide the whole pie, the smaller the pieces become?"

"Yes, ma'am," I lied.

The recess bell didn't ring for another half-hour and Mrs. Becker assigned twenty problems in our math book. Each problem was two fractions with an empty circle between. We were supposed to put a sign, > bigger than, or < smaller than, in each circle. Looking at all those fractions and circles made me dizzy. I decided I had a fifty/fifty chance of guessing which way to point the arrows, so I guessed.

After school when I got on-line with Joey I typed, "Flunked my math quiz today. I don't get fractions, how to tell which is bigger." Joey typed back, "Here's a good trick. Cross multiply." Then he showed me how.

$$\frac{2}{3} \ \& \ \frac{4}{5}$$

4/5 is larger than 2/3 because, '4' X '3' (12) is larger than '2' X '5' (10)

His trick made it a cinch, even for a dumbhead like me. This week when Mrs. Becker gave a fractions test, I was the only kid that got 100%. The class doesn't think I'm so stupid anymore, thanks to Joey.

After Joey and I got to be such good pals, I asked him to send me a picture. I told him I'd send him one of me. Our Little League team had our pictures taken in our uniforms. I posed for mine with my bat over my shoulder like I was up to the plate about to hit a home run. I thought I looked pretty cool – really athletic. I mailed one to Joey in Seattle, and started waiting for his picture to arrive in my mail.

Each day when we talked on the Internet, I asked him if he'd gotten my photo yet. On the third day he said, "Your picture came and it's awesome. Thanks!"

"Great!" I replied, "Then I should be getting yours soon." But Joey's picture never came, and each time we talked I told him, "Still no picture, maybe you'd better send another."

It was weird – no photo, and no comment from Joey. He'd just change the subject. Then one day when we were talking about *Star Wars* and aliens I asked him, "What if there really are aliens in disguise on earth? You know, like in the TV program *Third Rock From The Sun,* or the book, *My Teacher's An Alien?*"

It seemed like a long time before the screen lit

up with his reply.

"Can you keep a secret?"

"I guess," I answered.

"Promise? It's crucial!"

"Sure. I promise."

"I'm an alien from another galaxy. That's why I can't send a photograph to you. My energy field can't be caught on film."

I just sat there staring at the screen. My mother was calling me to dinner, and Joey signed off while I sat at the computer in a daze. Was this one of Joey's jokes? Then why didn't he send a picture? Why did he know so much more about space ships and outer space than other kids did? Why was he so secretive?

At dinner Dad announced, "Good news! My transfer request was approved. We'll be moving to the home office in Denver at the end of this month. The company has found a rental home for us that's close to a good school for Andy and with plenty of room for Grandma to live with us."

Mom was happy because her mother had been in a Denver nursing home ever since she fell and broke her hip, and she wanted to have Grandma live with us. Dad was happy because Marsten Mattress Manufacturers had transferred him to Portland, Oregon two years ago to set up a new plant and he couldn't wait to get back to Denver again. I just felt mixed up.

That night in bed, I thought about being a new kid in a new school. I remembered how I felt when we moved here. It seemed like everybody stared at me the first day, and the other kids treated me differently for a time until they got to know me.

Next morning, I was sitting at the kitchen table, eating my Cheerios while my mom was watching a show on TV. A newscaster was interviewing a lady in Seattle, Washington. "Tell me about the role the Internet plays in Joey's life?" the newscaster asked.

"Well, it has allowed him a freedom he's never known before. Not only is he able to access information from his wheelchair, but most importantly, he's made new friends."

The newscaster then asked, "Tell us about your Internet friends, Joey?" The camera shifted to this kid in a wheelchair, sitting in front of his computer. He was kind of skinny with sort of shriveled legs. His head hung to one side and when he answered, his words were hard to understand. He had to make a big effort to say them and a bit of drool came out one corner of his mouth.

"When other kids SEE me, they just see I'm different," Joey explained. "It's hard for me to talk and be understood, but easy for me to type on the computer."

All day at school my mind was a jumble of thoughts. Thoughts about my Internet pal, Joey. Joey, the alien. Joey, the kid on TV. Me, making new friends in Denver. Grandma, and her walker.

As soon as I got home, I ran to my room, threw my backpack on the bed, and went to my computer. As I logged onto the Internet, I decided it didn't matter where Joey came from – Mars, Saturn, or Seattle. It didn't matter what Joey looked like. I know who Joey is. He's my friend.

I typed into the computer. "Joey. Guess what? We're moving to Denver. Boy, am I ever glad to have a friend who goes with me wherever I go."

JOANNE PETERSON BIO

Joanne Peterson, who earned a B.A. in English Literature from The University of Washington, writes from her home in Sequim, Washington and continues to study the craft of writing through continuing education courses at the University of Washington and Peninsula College, the Pacific Northwest Writers' Association Conferences, Centrum Writers' Summer Workshop, and Olympic Field Seminar For Writers. She is affiliated with The Society of Children's Book Writers and Illustrators, Academy of American Poets, and the Pacific Northwest Writers' Association.

Joanne's poetry and short stories have appeared in journals and anthologies, including Poet's Guild, Poetry Northwest, Puget Soundings Magazine, Chicken Soup For The Soul, Mama Stew, and The California Quarterly. She has received contest awards from the Pacific Northwest Writer's Association and Writer's Digest (twice).

She has raised a family and engaged in business and continues to be involved with community service, education, the judicial system, and politics in the Seattle area. Extensive travel throughout the world has provided her with a deep appreciation of ethnic diversity.

Bunny Valentine
T. A. Taylor

Trevor burst into the kitchen with the grace of a rhinoceros on ice skates. When stocking feet meet linoleum, nothing good ever comes from it. Ducking, tucking and avoiding a nasty bump, he disappeared under the table, knocking away three chairs before stopping.

"Mom?" asked the voice under the table, "have you seen my Valentines?"

"In your backpack," answered Mother, repositioning the chairs.

Trevor stumbled clear and carefully maneuvered out of the kitchen. Finding his backpack by the front door, he knelt beside it, looked around to see if anyone was watching, then unzipped the middle compartment and checked the slot in the front; pulling a stack of envelopes from the secret pocket.

The stack was the essence of friendship. Each envelope painstakingly colored in shades of green with camouflage hearts. Meticulously addressed by Trevor with the names of his closest friends: Liam, Nick, Simon, Benjie, Lorenzo, and Billie. Billie hated to be called her real name, Willamina, especially by boys, who did not consider her a real girl. She could throw, kick, jump, run, and hit, harder, faster, higher, longer, and farther than any boy in class. But that's another story.

Trevor had picked out cool cards for all his friends. Each card had a paratrooper with a heart shaped parachute, camouflaged face, exclaiming, "HAPPY VALENTINE'S DAY" The inside read, "JUST WANTED TO 'DROP' IN AND SAY, YOU'RE SPECIAL!" Then he wrote, "Your friend, Trevor." His friends were going to love these cards, and he counted them.

One was missing! The card for Billie was not in the stack! Trevor quickly dipped his hand into the secret pocket and felt the missing envelope.

"Phew! That was close," sighed Trevor. "I wouldn't want to upset Billie by forgetting her Valentine."

He studied "WILLAMINA" blazoned in gold letters across the olive drab camouflaged envelope.

"I better fix this," thought Trevor heading back to the kitchen.

Mother was wiping down the table as Trevor climbed into a chair and asked for his crayons.

Setting the complete box in front of him, Mother inquired,

"Did you find all your cards?"

"Yes, ma'am, but I have to fix Billie's."

Trevor converted the "W" into a "B" and changed the "M" into an "I-E" then covered the remainder with his dark green crayon. Hardly noticeable unless one looked very closely.

"Listen Trev," Mother said, sitting down next to him. She always called him 'Trev' when she wanted a favor. It was usually something he would probably do without her asking, but he would never admit it.

"Yes, mother?" Trevor asked sarcastically.

"Trev, I think it's great you're sharing your commando cards with your friends."

"But?" giggled Trevor.

"But, can you take an extra card just in case some one doesn't get many? Know what I mean?"

"Kind of," Trevor answered, "If I didn't get any cards I might feel a little sad."

"Exactly!"

"But mom, I don't have any cards left, I barely had enough for my friends and I made a mistake on one and then you made me give one to the teacher."

"I know, Trev, that's why I picked up this Valentine card…"

"A BUNNY!" "Mom, I can't hand out a bunny card! How un-cool!"

"Trev, it's just in case; you can leave it in your bag where no one will see it. You don't even have to write your name on it, just sign it "your friend."

"M-o-o-o-o-om, if anyone sees me hand out this card I'll have to change schools."

"You won't have to change schools. Now go get your coat." She patted his bottom and he pretended his bottom hurt as he ran off.

In the classroom all the children hung up their coats and put their belongings in the closet. Trevor pulled out the camouflaged envelopes from his pack and counted them again. They were all there.

Mrs. Brodie entered with an exaggerated frown. Clapping her hands over the scrambling of small feet and high-pitched laughter, she addressed the class.

"Children, please. Find your seats, settle down Nick, and be seated," chided Mrs. Brodie. "We will pass out our Valentines, Jennifer, when everyone is sitting quietly and after we listen to the morning announcements. Not before, Simon, turn around and eyes forward please."

Some mornings Mrs. Brodie couldn't say a sentence without finding someone to use as an example... a practice that was very effective in bringing the class to a manageable level of chaos.

The morning announcements went as usual; Principal Plinkin was happy to announce that the school was performing some thing "really great" and doing another thing "exceptionally well" and the "hard work and dedication" of someone was still going on and on.

What actually was said was of little interest to Mrs. Brodie's second grade class, but they stared intently at the squawking box, anticipating the electronic crackle that signaled the end to this morning ritual.

"Have a great day!" and the box snapped silent.

This silence brought the class out of the hypnotic trance, and the second graders turned their eyes to Mrs. Brodie.

"Well," Mrs. Brodie stood, "Liam, sit up straight, please."

The class reacted as one as they all straightened their posture.

"Before we pass out our Valentines, remember to do it in an orderly manner, no running, no throwing, and Trevor, as little noise as possible, please."

Trevor smiled as he listened intently now, ignoring the faces Simon was making behind a shield of Valentine cards.

"You may place your Valentine Mailbags on your desks, and deliver your cards, Willamina, quietly."

With that, Mrs. Brodie rose from her desk and drifted through the rows, watching over the ensuing mayhem. The muffled giggles and shuffling feet added an acoustic rhythm to the dance of children delivering envelopes and smiles.

Trevor's mission: be the first card in all his friends' mailbags.

He quickly scurried up and down the rows, delivering his payload with the precision of an F-16 fighter. In just a matter of 60 seconds, he was back at his desk, basking in the glory of a mission accomplished.

Trevor peeked into the mailbag on his desk. He noticed a few cards had been tossed in. He dared not count how many. He did not want Mrs. Brodie to single him out for not waiting until lunch. So he waited and watched the other children.

Liam was shuffling between the desks, flipping through his envelopes to find a particular name, then he'd drop the lot of them. He'd pick them up and start all over. Trevor noticed the superhero envelopes and recognized it from inside his bag. He smiled knowing he was visited first by his best friend.

Billie stood in front of his desk. She slipped a card in his bag, smiled a grin minus a tooth, and skipped off.

Trevor noticed one child, however, in a slow methodical march from desk to desk. It was Marilyn Moore, and she would check the name on the bag and deposit the appropriate envelope. Trevor noticed that her progress was slow, but she smiled and moved happily from one desk to the next, passing no one.

Marilyn was new to class, joining at the end of January. She was quiet and kept to herself. Trevor had talked to her a few times but didn't really know much about her. He did know Marilyn talked in a low whisper of a voice.

The turbulence began to ebb, as more children settled into their seats. Trevor smiled contently and informed those around him that he was the first to be finished. He heard a rustle and the drop of a card into his Valentine Bag. Turning, Trevor witnessed Marilyn's smile as she turned and moved to the desk behind him. Trevor peered into his bag and on top was a princess envelope.

Marilyn gave him a card. That made him smile, but then he frowned. He hadn't thought to give a card to Marilyn. She was a girl, and he didn't know her that well, but she gave him a card. Trevor watched as Marilyn continued giving out her cards.

Trevor watched a few boys pass Marilyn's desk without stopping and then as a girl did the same. He wondered if anyone had given Marilyn a card. He slowly stood and drifted toward her desk; towards her mailbag.

"I thought you were finished!" harped Billie as Trevor flinched in surprise.

"I just, I mean, I am looking at the pretty hearts."

They were pretty... well drawn, vibrantly colored and adorning the bag atop Marilyn's desk. Flowers blooming at the top in yellow, green and red, welcomed all Valentines.

"I really think this bag is pretty, um, well drawn and, and, and pretty." Trevor nervously laughed hiding the fact that he took a quick peek inside and saw a dark empty contrast to the festive outside.

Billie smiled. "It is pretty."

She held up a card, gave Trevor a grin and dropped the card into Marilyn's bag.

Billie remembered Marilyn. Marilyn is getting at least one card, but only one. Trevor turned and saw Marilyn slowly making her way down the last row. He heard another card drop and he looked up to see that this one was from Mrs. Brodie.

"Trevor, if you are finished, please sit quietly like Nick."

Trevor looked and saw Nick straighten his posture; a role model to be emulated.

"I still have a card to get, Mrs. Brodie, I mean to give. It's in my bag."

Trevor turned for the closet and didn't look back. He hoped it was still there. He didn't notice it when he unpacked his other Valentines.

Marilyn was getting only two cards, and one was from the teacher!

Trevor had to do something. He checked the secret compartment of his backpack. Empty.

"I know it's here... I saw it... I ... put it... here."

There it was. All pink, soft and bunny like.

"Ugh..." whispered Trevor. "I'll put it in her bag, but I am not going to sign it."

Trevor opened the card and wrote "To a good friend, from a good friend" and stuffed the bunny card into the envelope.

"Whatcha doing?"

Trevor nearly jumped out of his skin.

"Liam! You sneak! Let someone know you're there will you?"

"And miss the cute wittle bunny," laughed Liam.

"It's not mine, it's for Marilyn. She doesn't have many in her bag."

"You're giving her a bunny card?"

"I didn't sign it, she won't know it's from me. Only you'll know and, as my best friend, you're sworn to secrecy. Remember the paste incident?"

Trevor never liked bringing up the paste incident because it was a dark chapter in Liam's life. Trevor also knew that not many other children remembered what happened that day, but Liam did.

"You got it, bud," said Liam; "I owe you big for keeping that one quiet. Do you think she'd like one of my cards?"

"You brought an extra card?"

"No, but I can give her the card I usually give myself."

"You give yourself a Valentine?"

"I'm not proud of it, but it's better than not getting any cards. If you think it'll make her happy, I'll part with it! Of course, this will be just between us."

"Of course, Liam and your sacrifice is greatly appreciated."

Trevor looked to see Marilyn halfway through the final row, her task nearing completion.

"We gotta hurry, Liam."

Liam ran to his bag and Trevor hid the pink soft envelope in his hands as he approached Marilyn's desk.

"No running, Liam. Sit quietly when finished."

With all eyes on Liam, Trevor dropped the

bunny card into Marilyn's bag and quietly made his way to his seat. Liam hastily dropped his card through the flowers atop Marilyn's Valentine Bag and was back in his seat before Mrs. Brodie could chastise him for running.

Marilyn, empty handed, crossed the room to take her seat and then all eyes fell upon Mrs. Brodie.

"Take your bags with you, do not open them until lunch. I will have no distractions, Willamina, and the other teachers won't as well. So, please, wait until lunch."

The bell rang and the children grabbed their bags and went to class. The morning dragged on, a fog to most, but when the lunch bell rang, a river of exuberance flowed through the halls. Trevor caught up to Liam.

"I thought you were ahead of me," huffed Liam. "I forgot my lunch," said Trevor.

As they walked into the cafeteria, they were awash in an energetic roar that reverberated off the tiled walls, mixed with bursts of laughter and echoes of conversations. They shuffled to their usual place, near the water fountain, and unpacked their delicacies; peanut butter and jelly crackers for Trevor, and a fried baloney and cheese toasted sandwich with a pickle for Liam.

"They're good," Liam responded to all who asked why he ate them, and nobody ever took Liam up on the offer to taste them. Trevor reasoned that Liam ate those sandwiches so that he wouldn't have to share his lunch. Trevor was very close to being correct.

Billie, with lunch tray, sat down. It was Tuesday, pizza day. Billie always bought her lunch on pizza day, with fries, applesauce, and chocolate milk. "Nice cards, boys," said Billie, "almost as many as I have."

"Thanks," said Trevor, "I got more than I expected."

"Your camouflaged cards are the coolest, Trevor", boasted Liam, boosting the ego of his buddy.

Liam then pretended the card was floating through the air, down to the table.

"Mayday, mayday, I'm bailing out over boloney island…"

Liam abruptly stopped as his card swooped in front of a lunch tray held by Marilyn. She sat down, smiling from ear to ear.

"Isn't it just a grand day?" asked Marilyn. "I see you have all your pretty cards out."

"We were just opening them up. How'd you do?" smiled Liam. Marilyn smiled back and pulled her flowery bag from her knapsack.

"I received four of the best cards. I'm not going to open them until I get home, so my mom can see them."

Trevor breathed easier not having to see the bunny card again as Marilyn continued.

"Mom told me not to expect many cards, being I'm so new here."

"Four's as many as I got." said Liam.

"Oh it's all just grand. I can't wait to share them with my Mom. She's been sad since we had to move in with Grandmom. I want her to see I made new friends and that I don't miss my old friends at the army base and that everything will be OK even though Daddy didn't come home."

Trevor and Liam sat quietly. Billie wiped something from her eye that she later would say was a chocolate milk drop. Trevor broke the silence pointing to the pink envelope in front of Marilyn and saying, "This one's from me."

The four roared with laughter and ate their lunches. Extraordinary children doing ordinary things.

T. A. TAYLOR BIO

T. A. Taylor grew up in the tumultuous sixties, in the New Jersey suburbs and then later in the outskirts of Baltimore, sheltered by parents from the onslaught of news.

Some may feel historically cheated, but he enjoyed a childhood for all it was worth, without a worry or care about growing up in a hostile world. Children need to be children for as long as they can be, unencumbered by adult reality that draws them away from childhood imagination.

He wants his stories to allow them to stay longer in such a place. If a little lesson can be slipped in now and then, that's even better.

"Extraordinary children doing ordinary things" expresses his belief that every child's story is a fascinating one.

An Odd Fable
Norma J. Sundberg

Far off in the land of Odd, atop a very round mountain, rests the realm of King Bing and Queen Irene. A moat surrounds the round kingdom, with the drawbridge always down to welcome wayfarers from other areas.

Because of the tremendous traffic over it, the drawbridge had developed dents and damaging holes, which not only made it treacherous to cross, but also threatened to cause it to collapse and cut off the Royal Family from the outside world. This caused a cloud of gloom to hang over the tiny kingdom. How sad. Then another vexing event occurred.

The land of Odd was so well rounded, so on the ball, so un-square that there were no sharp corners, no angles anywhere. At least there hadn't been—until one night with no one around, someone set a square table on the round ground of the downtown park, located at the precise central circle in the land of Odd.

Rumors flew of the strange square table downtown and soon people from every curve came to see the sight. What could it mean? The land of Odd was even odder than ordinary.

One day, King Bing queried the Queen: "Have you seen the White Knight, Irene?"

"The last time I spotted him he was headed downtown to the Round. That square table has caused quite a stir; it is an unequivocal curiosity."

"I must discuss the drawbridge with him. Those huge holes have been patched for several seasons and they just won't weld. We've tried everything but the kitchen sink," said the King.

"Oh! We tried that, too," continued the Queen, "When the new castle kitchen was installed, the cook hauled the old sink out there, but that didn't do, either. It fell right through into the water.

"We have to think of something soon," said the King. "As you well know, your mother, Grandmother Jolly, is due to visit."

Little Princess Giggle had slipped onto the scene as her parents were talking. She tugged at her father's sleeve and said, "Papa, I have an idea."

"Hush, little one," he said.

"But Papa, I have an idea, I have a good idea."

"Not now," said the King.

Giggle sighed and slid onto the seat of her unicycle and rode reluctantly out of the room.

"Be cheerful, Bing," cried the Queen, "We've always come through before. We will think of something."

"We'll consult the Knights," King Bing declared and made ready to ride downtown to the Round. Giggle begged to go too. She helped her papa prepare by hitching the ponies, Mercedes and Edsel, to their bright round cart and Giggle and the King climbed in. Queen Irene, who was terribly tired from hammering horseshoes and patching partitions of the pony cart all morning, said she would stay home. The little cart rattled and rumbled on its way, very carefully, across the dangerous drawbridge.

The little vehicle ventured toward the village. Soft wind sifted through Giggle's golden hair.

Her loosened sunbonnet hung down behind her coif of curls. The Princess held on to her hula-hoop hoping to have a happy afternoon.

The pony cart traversed the last turn and slowed to a stop. Giggle spotted the White Knight summoning them. He was her favorite, and the feeling was most mutual. Giggle's grin greeted him. Her blue eyes beamed as her Knight came near. He lifted her elfin lightness, happily hugging her.

"Well little one," he said, "Do you plan to use that hula-hoop to help hide those hideous holes?"

She giggled, "You're silly." The little Princess wriggled down and pranced off to play, her pinafore tails trailing behind her. She set her hula-hoop around the flowers in one of the round gardens, and carefully picked several perfect posies, placing them in her pocket. She picked a pink one to put in her papa's lapel.

The King's gaze followed her fondly. Then he saw several of the Knights noticing the square table; watched as one ran his fingers over the shiny surface, while another looked underneath to see how it was constructed. Still another sat on one of the attached benches.

Once they caught the King's eye, they hastily worked their way to the Round Table.

All the town's meetings and business sessions were held in the Round. There was even theater in the Round. But on this day the presence of that peculiar square table was a distraction to the dignitaries. Each eyed it as the council convened.

The group gathered, including: The White Knight, who stood sturdy and straight, even when he wasn't wearing his armor; and two new Knights, twin sisters, Holly and Hilda. It was the first time siblings had been selected to sit in the King's Court.

Finally, there was Dismal Knight, with tarnished gray armor and rust rings here and there, saying,

"Harrumph, harrumph, your plans will never work."

Each of the Knights took turns telling what they would do to fix the deficient drawbridge. "We suggest," said Holly and Hilda in unison, "that we fill in the moat and plant gardens around the castle, then you wouldn't need a drawbridge."

"Harrumph," said Dismal Knight, "There isn't enough earth in the whole area to fill in the moat; it will never work!"

"Besides," added Giggle, who had slipped into the center of the curious congregation, "Grandfather Jolly enjoys fishing in the moat and Grandma Jolly loves to dangle her feet in the water on a hot day."

"Harrumph," echoed Dismal Knight.

The White Knight sent forth his suggestion.

"Is it possible to have an architect design a better bridge?"

"Costs too much," groaned the King.

"What about a fair to raise revenue?" the White Knight continued.

The King countered, "We just had a fair for the renovation of the Round. That is the real reason for the strange sight of that terrible table. The object, obviously, was out of order from its origin."

No one said another word. Giggle tiptoed over and tugged at her father's sleeve, "Papa, Papa, I have an idea. I have a good idea."

The King didn't listen. "Papa, Papa," she said again, "I have an idea. I have a good idea."

"Just one moment Giggle, just one moment," continued the King.

"But Papa, you're not being fair! Why you've always told me every person should be able to speak in parliamentary procedure, but you won't let me!"

She stomped her foot.

"Let Giggle speak, your Highness, said the White Knight, "Children are often sources of sound sense."

"Let Giggle speak," said Holly and Hilda, "Let Giggle speak," echoed the rest, including Dismal Knight. King Bing lifted Giggle onto the bench beside him.

"Tell me your good idea."

"Why don't you set the square table over the moat? It would fit, I'm sure, and it would last a long time. Besides, if the benches were kept on either edge, Grandmother Jolly could dangle her feet in comfort."

"Eureka!" cried the White Knight, as he picked Giggle up, shifting her to his shoulder.

"My word," commented the King.

"By jove, she's solved it," chorused Holly and Hilda in unison.

"Harrumph," said Dismal Knight, I think her idea is ideal. I think it will work."

So the bright new bridge was installed, complete with ribbon-ripping rite and all. However, the people of Odd had grown so accustomed to the square table that they missed it in the Round. Being a liberated realm, the people proposed the purchase of a new square table. So it was done and even Dismal Knight was satisfied with the result and the King was so pleased when the new bridge was set in place and a new square table graced the Round that he made Giggle Odd's official tour guide.

Every day from ten to four, following her daily tutoring, she drives the nifty new horse-drawn 'Odd Trolley' tour bus, complete with soft round doughnut tires, pulled by two marvelous mares, and shows visitors 'Giggle Bridge', named after herself. She introduces them to Grandfather Jolly fishing and Grandma Jolly wiggling her toes in the smooth water.

But perhaps the happiest sight of all is Dismal Knight, quite cheerful as he gazes about murmuring,

"A square bridge, who would have thought! A veritable innovation!"

And quite often all the Knights invite Giggle to the square table in the Round to share a peaceful picnic.

NORMA J. SUNDBERG BIO

For ten of the forty-something (almost 50) years of writing and publishing, Norma J. Sundberg composed a weekly column for a small Ohio newspaper, penning take-offs on family life with ten children. After returning to college in mid-life to earn an AA degree, she taught poetry to young people in College for Kids; co-authored (as poet), with Claudia Greenwood Ph.D., a manual for non-traditional women returning to college.

Then Norma ran away from home and continues to chase the muse in Tallahassee, FL, publishing poetry and essays in little and literary magazines and keeping in close contact with other writers. This is her first children's story.

Recently, she attended the Erma Bombeck Humor Writers' Conference in Dayton, Ohio and has an article in the November 04 Newsletter on the Humor Writers Workshop website.

The Monster Down the Street
Almondie Shampine

We walked by the house probably three or
four times a day, slowing our pace to glance in
through the windows and gaze longingly at the
old, rusty swing set. The place looked vacant, like
someone hadn't lived there for years. Weeds that
nearly reached our bellies filled the small yard,
and the once gravel driveway was lost in crab
grass. Sycamore trees given too much freedom
branched out over the house, shading it from the
sunlight and adding to its already scariness.

We never saw any lights on or anyone come and go. We never saw a moving shadow when the sun was setting just right and shone light into the two front windows, but from talk in the schoolyard during fourth grade recess, someone lived there, but who? "Can't be human," Carrie whispered. We were standing in front of the old, yellowing house, as we did often.

"No, definitely not," I agreed. "What do you think it is?" she asked. "I don't know." I kept my eyes fixed on the broken screen door. Hanging from only one rusty hinge, it creaked as the cool breeze pushed it back and forth, back and forth. "Something that lives in the dark," I said.

"With eyes that glow like flashlights."

"All alone."

"Doesn't need to leave the house to go grocery shopping because it eats spiders and beetles and ants."

"Just gobbles them up with no teeth."

"Except for two fangs to pin them down and suck their blood."

"It crawls around on its four claws."

"With long, sharp, green nails."

"Bloodstains on the tips."

"And it's hairy, like a bear, like a ... a ... monster!" Carrie said, reaching for my hand.

BANG! The broken screen door burst open and slammed into the porch railing. We scampered off squealing like pigs in trouble.

Summer came round, meaning an extra eight hours of playtime every day. We tried to keep ourselves busy doing other things like playing countless games of basketball, kickball, and base-ball, and zooming through the Deer Run trailer park streets on our bicycles, but something kept us going back to the house everyday. The ground had become a raw brown from where we always stood, fifty feet away from the answers to our constant, quiet questions.

Maybe it was harmless curiosity, or the fact that neither Carrie nor I had a swing set, so the swings at the house looked like so much fun, if only we could play on them, or maybe it was simply knowing that we didn't know everything that led us to do what no kid had ever dared to do before. All I know is I'll never forget the events that followed once we knocked on that old, wooden door.

It was another boring day in Central Square, New York. I'd awakened to dark clouds and depressing rain, spent the morning reading, the noon hour dozing in front of the television, and the early afternoon staring out the window and loudly moaning my boredom.

"Joann, why don't you call Carrie and see what she's doing," Mom suggested. I think she just wanted me to stop whining about being so bored.

Ten minutes later, I was out the door and walking to my best friend's house. The sky was still dark, and the breeze was moist and cold, but the rain had stopped for now.

"So, what do you wanna do?" she asked. "I don't know," I shrugged. We sat on her porch steps, licking our berry popsicles in silence.

"Do you think maybe it's lonely?" I asked suddenly. "What?"

"The monster. It sits in that house all day in the dark all alone. Maybe it just needs a friend," I said. "Yea, to eat for dinner," Carrie laughed.

"Let's go see if we can see it through the window." "But we never do," she whined.

And there we were, once again, gawking at the house, wondering the same things.

"Look, Carrie, a light," I gasped. A dim light shone through one of the small windows, but the window was too high for us to get a good look at the inside of the house.

"Boy, those swings look like awful fun," Carrie said. "It's too wet out to play kickball, and if we ride our bikes, we'll get muddy. If only we could just swing on those swings. We'd never be bored again."

"I'm gonna go ask it if we can play on its swings," I said. My fear was great, but my curiosity and boredom were greater.

"What? You're ... You're crazy!" she whispered fearfully. "You'll get kidnapped and ... and eaten. You'll be killed. Remember what Tommy Thompson said, Joann? Anyone who goes up those steps never comes back. Tommy's in the sixth grade, so he knows," she warned me.

I started for the yard. "Joann!" she cried.

"Carrie, if it hates children so much, why does it have a swing set?" I reasoned with her.

"To get kids to come into his yard to eat them, just like robbers use candy to kidnap kids," she answered.

I paused halfway through the tall, sticky weeds. I was having second thoughts, thinking that maybe this wasn't such a grand idea after all. No, I'd gotten this far. I was in the middle of a mission and I was not a quitter.

"Or maybe he just wants a friend, but everyone else is too much of a scaredy pants to knock on the door," I said.

"I'm not scared," she stood up for herself.

"Yes you are," I challenged her.

"No I'm not. I'll knock on that door myself." She stubbornly trampled through the lawn, pausing beside me.

We tiptoed toward the house, hearts pounding, and bodies shaking. We grasped for one another's hand and started up the creaky steps.

"We both will," she said. We lifted our trembling fists and softly knocked on the paint-chipped door.

We heard something! SQUEAK! SQUEAK! The doorknob rattled as it turned. The door groaned as it slowly ... slowly ... opened.

We were ready to bolt like lightning, maybe even faster than that. I couldn't move my eyes from the door.

...Slowly ... slowly ... "AAAAAAAH!" we shrieked. "Wait, you're not a monster." I stopped screaming.

"Did you think I was a monster?" The old, bald man with the bright blue eyes smiled at us.

"Everyone does. We thought you were a big, hairy monster that ate children, not an old Grandpa," Carrie admitted.

73

"Carrie!" I elbowed her.

"Well, I do like children for dinner," he said.

"Really?" My eyes got wide in fright.

"Well of course. There's nothing like having company to help me eat all my food," he told us.

My shoulders fell in relief. For a moment, I'd thought he was really going to eat us.

"We don't like bugs," Carrie said.

He laughed, coughed real hard, and then turned serious. "You human beings don't like bugs?" he teased. "Yuck!" We stuck our tongues out.

"What about dirt? You like to eat dirt?"

"Gross!" we shouted.

"Hmm! Well, I do have some chocolate chip cookies fresh out of the oven, but I don't think..."

"Yeeeah!" we screamed excited.

"Why don't you ever leave the house?" Carrie asked him.

"I can't get around like I use to," he said, nodding his head down toward his wheelchair. That's why we could never see him through the windows.

He rolled into the kitchen, and every time the left wheel went round, it squeaked.

"Why don't you ever have any lights on?" I asked, looking around the dark house. The kitchen light was on, but it wasn't very bright.

"I'm an old man. It hurts my eyes."

After filling up on cookies and milk and promising to eat dinner when we got home, we ran out to finally play on the swing set. It was old and rusty and the chains whined a whole lot, but it didn't matter to us. Flying through the air, kicking our feet out, leaning forward, and jumping into the fluffy weeds, there wasn't a better feeling in the entire world.

We still wondered why an old man would have a swing set. Then he told us it had once been his daughter's and that she and his wife were now in heaven with God to watch over them.

Everyday that summer, we went to the house. We would help him clean and keep him company and he would always have some kind of delicious treat for us to munch on. Kids walking by and riding by on their bicycles would stare at us and quietly warn us about waking the monster. We never told them there was no monster, only a nice, old man who couldn't get around much. Heck if we were gonna share our goodies and swings!

Then one day at the end of summer, he sat us down at his small, wooden table and said, "I'm going away soon, girls." "Where you going?" I asked with my mouth full of apple.

"I miss my wife and daughter. It's time I go where they are," he smiled softly.

"In heaven?" I asked. He nodded his head.

"Can we come? We'd like to meet your wife and daughter, Mr. Shoop."

He laughed. "That's very sweet of you, little Carrie, but you won't see them or me, again, for many, many years. Now, I just want to thank you girls for giving me peace and happiness these past couple months. Before you ladies came along, I was very sad and lonely. You gave back to me what I'd lost years ago when my two precious loves died, my wife and daughter."

"What else had you lost, Mr. Shoop, that we could help you find?" Carrie asked.

"My smile," he answered. "Even though I'll be gone, the swing set is yours to play with whenever you want." "Thank you, Mr. Shoop," we said, but we didn't really understand.

He kissed our foreheads and sent us off to play on the beloved swing set.

We never did see Mr. Shoop again, but we'll never forget him. His swing set kept us busy and having fun on what otherwise would have been boring days, and no one could make chocolate chip cookies like he had made.

ALMONDIE SHAMPINE BIO

My mother named me after the candy bar, Almond Joy. I currently live in Chadwicks, New York with my two-year-old son and his future sibling still fresh in my womb. I am 21 years old, have been writing for nine years, and plan to do so for as long as I continue to dream restlessly at night.

Aside from writing, I enjoy singing and anything that will get my hands dirty and feeling a youth that is taken so early in a child's life.

'The Monster Down the Street' was inspired by my own childhood.

The Truth And Other Rumours
Karen Kirkconnell

Note: Where authors have used non-standard
US spellings, we have left that form.

There's a rumour going 'round my school
    And I don't think it's funny.
A bunch of kids are saying that
    My family's got no money.

They don't know my mom gave up her job
    To go to school to make things better,
That I haven't seen my Dad since I was two,
    Not a phone call or a letter.

Hey …
    I know what to do!

"Let me set you straight, you guys,
    Since you really seem to care.
First, about my absent Dad . . .
    The AS-TRO-NAUT MILL-ION-NAIRE!"

"He's on a lengthy mission,
    Leading a space crew 'round the
stars.
We expect he'll land next April
    Once he's spent some time on
Mars."

77

"And he promised to bring me back a chunk
  Of each planet that he lands on.
He took a special space-safe trunk
  The biggest he could get his hands on."

"Then there's what you've all been saying
  About my mom and me.
Let me just start by telling you
  There's WAY more than you see."

"At first glance you think I'm just a boy
  Who doesn't have enough.
But at my other house . . . in HOLL-Y-WOOD
  There're tons and TONS of stuff."

"See, I'm not the kid you think I am.
  I'm just in town to learn a part.
I'm doing research on a character . . .
  A boy who's poor but has a heart."

"Yes, I'm a very famous actor,
  As I'm sure by now you've guessed.
You've no doubt seen my movies.
  Fifteen in all, this one's the best."

"My newest film's a real sad tale.
  This poor boy, the others tease him
About his clothes, his hair, his life . . .
  There's just no way that he can please them."

"His poor mother works both night and day,
    But it never seems to affect her.
She smiles and shows her son such love . . .
    Did I mention my own mother's the director?

"So thank you all for helping me out.
    I've really learned a thing or two
About feeling hurt and left out just because
    I'm not as rich as you."

"YOU'RE LYING," shouted Billy Green,
    "I DON'T BELIEVE A WORD YOU'VE
SAID!
Your Dad just left, he's not in space,
    The whole story is all in your head."

"Yeah," said Thomas, "Let's go, you guys."
    And he turned to walk away.
"You're not famous, you're nothin' at all"
    He turned back to me to say.

I fought back my tears and turned to go
    When a girl with glasses and frizzy hair
Spoke in the loudest voice she'd ever used . . .
    "DON'T . . . YOU . . . DARE!!!"

Everyone stopped dead in their tracks.
    I thought she was talking to me,
But when I looked at her she was glaring at them
    And she shouted, "DON'T YOU SEE?"

"Sure, he made up all that stuff
    And told fat lies aplenty.
But behind each one were some
    Sad truths 'bout us - you and me."

"Forget the movie thing and Space Man Dad,
    And hear what he really said out loud.
Behind the lies lives a sad, sad boy,
    And I can tell you, I'm not proud."

"We've treated him like he's second rate
    Because of things that just don't matter.
What if you were teased by the rest of us
    For being thinner, taller or fatter."

"I'm sorry for how we treated you,"
    She turned to me to say.
"I hope you know you can just be yourself,
    that from A to Z, you're O.K."

Then this girl, she went all quiet,
    No one knew where to begin.
We all just stood there, mouths agape,
    You could have heard the drop of a pin.

Until a small boy at the back of the group
    Started clapping. It got everyone going.
Even Billy and Thomas joined in the applause
    Nothing but good feelings were flowing.

So, while things in my life haven't changed much,
    My mom and me are still just getting by,
And my Dad, he's still pretty much out of my life
    I don't feel ashamed and I don't have to lie.

That day, we learned about caring,
    Beyond what we learn in our classes.
We learned how to make this a better place
Thanks to a frizzy-haired girl with glasses.

KAREN KIRKONNEL BIO

Karen holds a Master's degree in Clinical Psychology and has worked in the field of child and family therapy for nearly twenty years, primarily with children and adults who had experienced emotional trauma. Storytelling has always been a big part of her clinical work, and that, together with a story-enriched Scottish heritage and an eager audience in her own two young children, led her to turn her hand to writing in 2001.

In addition to editing and writing for a community newspaper, Karen has had her work published in The Globe and Mail newspaper, the Canadian Authors' Association poetry chapbook and in an anthology of essays entitled, *Facts and Ar-*

guments: A selection of essays from the Globe and Mail (Penguin Press, 2002).

More recently, Karen returned to school to study education and is currently an elementary school teacher. Stories continue to be a passion in her life. Karen lives with her husband, Ross, and her two children, Andrew and Katie, in Guelph, Ontario, Canada. Their cat, Sebastian, comes and goes.

Miranda And The Dark Forest
Julia Wight

Miranda and her younger brother Joshua lived with her parents in a house at the edge of a dark forest.

"You must never go into the forest," said her father.

"Why?" said Miranda. "Because it's a very dangerous place," said her mother.

"Dangerous? I think it looks beautiful."

"Well," said her father, "Long ago before you could remember, you had a sister named Tabitha.

She wandered off into the forest. We looked and looked for her, but we never saw her again."

"Oh, no," said Miranda, her heart pounding. "Why didn't you tell me I had a sister?"

"We didn't want to tell you, because it would make you unhappy. Now you see why you must never go there," said her mother, through her tears.

"I promise," said Miranda. *But when I'm older I will go and find my sister,* she thought to herself.

One day, her parents went to visit her sick grandmother who lived in the nearby town.

"Miranda, please keep an eye on your brother until we return," said her father.

"Yes, Daddy." She liked being asked to look after her brother as it made her feel grown up.

"Don't forget what we told you," said her mother, "Keep an eye on your brother, and never ever go into the forest."

"We'll be back before dark," said her father.

"Please don't worry," said Miranda, "Joshua's wearing such a bright red sweater, he'll be easy to watch."

Miranda waved goodbye to her parents. The sun warmed her face, as she listened to the sound of birds and rustling trees.

She watched her brother in his red sweater, busy with a trowel, shoveling dirt into a small green wheelbarrow. She started to sing and dance around the garden, pretending she was a fairy queen. Joshua kept on digging.

"Whew, I'm hot," she said. "And so thirsty, I'll just get us both a drink of water." She went into the kitchen, turned on the faucet, and let the water run cool and fresh before she filled her glass. Then she drank and drank, until her parched mouth was soothed.

Back to the garden to check on that little brother of mine, and give him a glass of water.

"Joshua, Joshua, where are you?" I bet he's hiding, the little devil.

"O.K. Joshua, come out from wherever you are."

The sun slipped behind a cloud. The birds were silent. Not a leaf stirred. She felt a faint shiver down her spine. How could she feel so cold? The glass slipped from her hand shattering to smithereens. The trowel was lying between two rhododendron bushes at the end of the garden, just at the edge of the forest.

"He's gone and it's all my fault," she said, tears springing to her eyes." I must find him, even if it means going in there." She picked up the trowel, took a deep breath, and walked straight into that dreaded place.

Huge trees, like menacing monsters, surrounded her on every side. No sunlight reached the branches. No birds sang.

Something red was lying on the ground. Was it a wilted blossom? It was yarn from Joshua's sweater. The yarn ran ahead of her like red spaghetti.

This yarn will lead me to Joshua. She felt her heart racing. She picked up the unraveled end and started to wind it around the trowel. Then she continued, going deeper and deeper into the forest.

Suddenly, the end of the yarn appeared.

"Oh, no, now what will I do? I am completely lost. Oh, why did I leave my brother alone? I only left him for a minute."

Miranda threw herself onto a pile of dried leaves. She started to sob as if her heart would break. Finally, exhausted, she fell asleep.

Swoosh! Swoosh! She opened her eyes, looked up, and saw a woman holding a broomstick. She wore a long purple dress with a black flowing cloak that fluttered all by itself without the aid of any wind.

"Well my dear," said the woman, "My name is Hagatha, head witch of this forest."

Miranda stood up, brushing the leaves from her sweater. "How do you do," said Miranda, in amazement.

"As we witches keep a close ear to the ground, our telegraph informs me your brother has been kidnapped by Malatha."

"Who's Malatha?" said Miranda.

"She's an evil witch, a total undesirable, and adds nothing to the community. I blame myself. When she arrived I did not check her credentials carefully enough. In fact, I hear she kidnaps children so she can fatten them up for dinner or use them as slaves."

"Oh, no," said Miranda, her eyes opening wide.

"Only you can help us rid the forest of this vile pest," said Hagatha.

"How?" said Miranda. "What about my brother?"

"First, you will rescue your brother. Then we can use you as a witness at her trial. We must prove to the Mighty Warlock of the East that she is guilty of kidnapping children, so he will banish her for ever."

"Oh, my!" said Miranda. "I have to find my brother and get home before dark. My parents will be so worried."

"Not a problem, my dear. We witches can manipulate time, so your parents won't even know you've left the house. We are wasting valuable time. Your mission is to rescue your brother. Good luck."

"Thank you," said Miranda. "But how?"

"Let me see my dear," said Hagatha. She tapped the ground three times with her right foot. "Liver of toad, eye of newt, blood of bat, grant my wish or I'll eat my hat." Poof! A swirl of orange and green smoke made Miranda sneeze.

"Aha!" said Hagatha, plucking a broomstick out of the smoke. "This is a deluxe model. It will hold up to three children. All you have to do is sit on it, and make a wish. It will take you wherever you want. But remember, use it wisely."

Zoom! Zoom! Hagatha disappeared before Miranda could say goodbye. She sat sideways on the broomstick, held on tight, and closed her eyes.

"Take me to my brother."

Whoosh! Wheesh! She opened her eyes feeling the wind on her face. Down, down she went and found herself outside a cottage surrounded by birch trees. Huge vultures gazed down at her from the thatched roof.

She leaned the broom against the cottage and peeked into an open window. There, she saw Joshua sitting in a chair, his eyes glazed over.

Then Malatha stormed into the room, smoke pouring from her nostrils, her face the color of turkey giblets. She was clutching an enormous plate of chocolate cake and ice cream.

"Here, give this to the boy," she bellowed to a girl dressed in rags stirring a huge cauldron. Malatha grabbed Joshua and threw him into a large cage. The girl followed Joshua into the cage with the plate. He gulped down the chocolate cake and ice cream as if he hadn't eaten for days.

"That's right, eat up," cackled the witch, as she locked the cage, " I like fat, juicy little boys."

Suddenly, the witch saw Miranda looking through the window. She started to shake and fell to the floor with green and yellow foam coming out of her mouth. Then she stopped moving.

I wonder if she's dead. It's no good being scared; I have to rescue Joshua and that poor girl. Miranda crept around to the front door, lifted the latch, and peered inside. She looked into the cage at the ragged girl and stopped in stunned surprise. The witch still lay sprawled in front of the cage.

"I know who you are," said Miranda. "You're my twin sister Tabitha."

Tabitha gasped! "My dream has finally come true," said Tabitha, her eyes sparkling. "Look at this locket with our baby pictures. I always knew that my twin sister would rescue me." Tears started streaming down her face.

"So that's why the witch got such a fright. She thought I was you," said Miranda. Miranda spotted the key beside the witch's body. "Let's get you both out of here," she said, unlocking the cage.

"Look out, the witch is moving," said Tabitha, her eyes opening wide in terror.

"Quickly," said Miranda. "Take our brother out by the backdoor, bring the broomstick and come around to the front. As soon as I tie this red yarn across the threshold of the front door, I'll call her. We can trip her and tie her up."

"But how can we escape?" said Tabitha.

"No problem. The broomstick can easily take the three of us out of here," said Miranda. With her heart pounding, Miranda raced to the door and tied the yarn to two bushes growing on either side. Then she knocked as hard as she could.

Knock! Knock!

"Who's there? said Malatha.

"It's me, you ugly old sourpuss," yelled Miranda. She opened the door and stuck out her tongue.

"Wait 'til I get my hands on you," roared the horrible hag, smoke coming from her nostrils, her face the color of eggplant. As she crossed the threshold, she tripped over the red yarn, crashing to the ground.

"Quick, help me tie her up," said Miranda, as she stuck a wad of yarn in the witch's mouth.

With trembling hands, Tabitha bound the ankles while Miranda secured the wrists.

"Jump on!" said Miranda, astride the broomstick. Taking Joshua's hand, Tabitha managed to scramble aboard.

"Now, let's get out of here," said Miranda, "And on to the next valley." Vroom! Vroosh!

"Good job," came a familiar voice. It was Hagatha on her broomstick. "The Great Warlock of the East has sent his army to catch Malatha. Now children, follow me to the court of the Great Warlock. We will see justice done. Miranda, my dear, you have saved the day for your sister and brother and all the good witches in the forest."

"Where am I?" said Joshua, rubbing his eyes." Where's my sweater?"

"One moment, please," said Hagatha. She shook her right foot three times. "Deadly nightshade, ivy, yew, grant that the sweater is made anew." Poof! A puff of red smoke covered the children for an instant.

"You're wearing it," said Miranda with a chuckle. "Yippee!" said Joshua.

"Look at me," said Tabitha, "I've got brand new clothes."

"Just like mine," said Miranda. "Now we really are twins. Hold on tight, here we go."

Vroom! Vroosh! And they were off.

"There's Hagatha," said Tabitha, pointing to a grassy hill below them. "Whee!" said Joshua, as the broom nose-dived and landed beside Hagatha.

"This way children," said Hagatha, pointing to an opening in the side of the hill. They entered a tunnel lit by flaming torches. The shadows from the flames danced on the walls like jungle grass. A bat skimmed overhead. Hagatha opened a huge oak door at the end of the tunnel.

They had arrived at the Court of the Great Warlock of the East. Clinging to each other, the children followed Hagatha into the court. The great hall appeared to be bathed in moonlight.

Bats and owls swooped above them in the rafters of the cavernous ceiling. Witches and warlocks laughed and chatted like parents at a PTA meeting.

At the far end of the great hall stood an enormous wooden screen carved with fantastic creatures. To the left sat a group of witches and warlocks.

"That must be the jury," said Tabitha in a whisper. "Welcome," boomed a voice that appeared to be coming from behind the screen. The children trembled.

"Greetings, Great Warlock," said Hagatha. "I have brought your chief witness, the brave Miranda."

"Bring in the prisoner," said the booming voice. The great hall went silent as Malatha entered the court bound in chains.

"You are charged with kidnapping and enslavement of innocent children. How do you plead?" said the Great Warlock.

"Not guilty," said Malatha, as her mottled face turned from red to purple.

"My sister saved me from that horrible monster," said Tabitha, pointing her finger at Malatha. "Me too," said Joshua jumping up and down.

Miranda trembled with fright but stood up and told her story.

"Members of the jury, how do you find the defendant?" said the Great Warlock.

"Guilty as charged," said the foreman of the jury.

"Liars! Liars! screamed Malatha shaking her fist. Green foam started coming out of her mouth and nostrils.

"You are banished for ever to the Desert of the Dinosaur Bones beyond the mountains. Take her away."

"Hooray for Miranda," said Hagatha waving her broomstick in the air. "Hooray for Miranda," echoed around the courtroom.

"In honor of your great bravery, Miranda, I wish to bestow on you the order of the Great Warlock of the East," said the invisible warlock.

Hagatha stepped forward and draped a purple sash over Miranda's head and across her shoulder.

"Thank you," said Miranda. She felt her heart opening up like a sunflower turning its face to the sun.

"You won't need this anymore," said Hagatha, as she took the broomstick from Miranda's hand. Hagatha stamped her foot three times. "Time to go/no more to roam/send these children to their home." A cloud of blue and purple smoke descended on the children.

"I can't see," said Joshua. When the air cleared, they were standing in their back yard.

"We're home, but no one's here," said Miranda. The children stood hand in hand. They turned to watch the sunset behind the dark silhouettes of the tall fir trees, a blaze of orange and red across the sky.

"I'm tired," said Tabitha with a yawn. "I'm hungry," said Joshua.

Toot! Toot! Their parents drove up the driveway.

"They're home!" yelled Miranda. The children rushed to greet them.

"I can't believe my eyes," said their mother, leaping from the car.

"Neither can I," said their father, as he raced towards them. The parents and children clung to each other. Nobody wanted to let go.

"I rescued Tabitha," said Miranda. Her heart swelled with pride.

"Don't forget me," said Joshua.

"Oh, well done my brave Miranda. My dream of finding Tabitha came true," said their mother.

"Now we're family again," said their father, his arms wrapped around the group of huggers.

"I'm hungry," said Joshua. "Time for dinner," said their mother. She wiped away her tears and laughed.

The silver moonlight caressed the needles of the tall fir trees. An owl with outstretched wings flew across the moon in ghostly silence.

Hagatha stood outside, and watched the family around the dinner table. Was there ever a braver girl than Miranda? She will always have a place in this old witch's heart. She looked up at her old friend the moon.

"Well, time to leave so I can keep watch over this forest," she said in a whisper.

Whoosh! Zoom! And then, S-I-L-E-N-C-E

JULIA WIGHT BIO

Julia and her twin sister were born in England in 1945 to an English mother and Czech father. When she was six months old, the family moved to her father's hometown of Bruntal, Silesia in Czechoslovakia, known as the Sudetenland under the Third Reich. There her brother was born in 1948, the year of the Communist takeover. The family was lucky enough to get out the following year and make its way to England, living near London. In 1955, they moved to Ireland and lived in Howth, on the North end of Dublin Bay.

At 18, Julia left Ireland, went to Paris and lived with a French family for five months. She then went to London to study Montessori education, which led her to a 20-year education career in the United States. After living in Panama for the last 10 years, she went to Seattle and turned to writing. She took the certificated program for Children's Writing and the on-line Fiction Writing Program at the University of Washington. Julia and her husband of 35 years live on Puget Sound with stunning views of the Olympic Mountains.

Artwork by Wendy Wolf

Brown Eyes
Wendy Wolf

There once was a community of children who divided themselves into groups according to the color of their eyes.

The blue-eyed children formed one group and played only with each other. The green-eyed children gathered together, and spoke only among themselves. The brown-eyed children separated as well, and drew imaginary lines to keep the others out.

Children with eyes of uncommon colors like hazel, gray, violet, pink, and black, formed another group, and bonded with the common element of uncommonness.

All was peaceful as long as no one crossed over the lines into the groups of others to talk or play.

Until one day, a child from the brown-eyed group saw the green-eyed children playing a game she did not know, and she wanted to join them. This had not been done since before the color lines had been drawn.

The green-eyed children argued among themselves about what to do. Some saw no harm in letting the brown-eyed girl play with them. "Why not?" they shrugged.

"Because she's not like us," the others protested.

"So?"

But the children who wanted to keep the color lines intact were loud and strong. "NO!" they cried. "She can't play with us. She isn't like us, and those are the rules."

"Who made the rules?" one of the children asked. "And why can't we change them?"

"Because," the others shouted. The truth was that no one really knew the reason.

So, the group broke in two, while the other children watched in shocked fascination.

The brown-eyed girl quietly backed away from the argument and returned to the other brown-eyed children. She never meant to cause a fight.

Now she was no longer welcome there. "You crossed the line. You're brown. They're green.

They aren't like us, and now we know you're not like us, either. Go away. You have no place here."

All alone, she blinked back tears. It made no sense. *What does color matter?* she thought. *We're all different... straight hair, curly hair, short, tall, brown skin, pale. We're all just children... we're all the same that way.*

Sad tears streamed from her eyes, because now, she was the *most* different. She was a group of one.

Just then, the green-eyed children who wanted to allow her into their group came to form a circle around her. They held hands and sang.

The other groups who had watched the conflict in silence began to express opinions of their own. Those who thought the color rule was silly joined hands with the children in the circle, and they sang, too.

The brown-eyed girl dried her eyes, and walked to a place in the circle that had opened up for her. She joined hands with the other children, and they all sang together.

The circle grew, and soon *it* became the largest group.

The color groups were quite small now. Most of the children had already joined the circle. Meanwhile, the singing continued.

Finally, the remaining children outside of the circle began to hum along. They approached the others certain they would be turned away, but to their great surprise, a gray-eyed boy and a green-eyed girl dropped hands and reached out to them.

They held the outstretched hands, and beaming brightly, sang loudly and quite off key. The sound was beautiful.

The sun shone on them all day, and the stars twinkled above them all night.

All was peaceful again... and a lot more fun.

Editorial Note: Stories for **Beyond Time and Place** were numbered for blind judging so it came as a surprise that four authors had each written two winning stories

For WENDY WOLF BIO, see next story

Artwork by Wendy Wolf

The Wall
Wendy Wolf

Every day, on her way to school, Mika passed a long, low concrete wall. It was covered in graffiti, painted in careless anger by a group of restless teenagers. Mika held her breath whenever she walked by it.

One day, she decided to make the wall more beautiful. Squatting on the ground beside it on her way home from school, she unpacked a small set of paints she had borrowed from art class. She painted a daisy with white petals and a yellow center, and leaves that reached toward the sky. When she was done, she felt hopeful. It was a small start, but a start nonetheless.

Each day after that one, Mika added a new flower or a bee or a butterfly to the wall in between the dark slashes of black and red paint put there previously. A week passed, and a small garden began to emerge.

Her classmates noticed the project, and word spread throughout the school. When Mika's art teacher, Miss Riemer, heard about it, she called Mika into her office. She leaned against her desk, arms folded, and said, "I love that you're doing this. Can I help?"

Mika nodded her head with enthusiasm. "Yes!" she said. "I was running low on paint, anyway...and the wall is so big!" Miss Riemer smiled, and that afternoon, she circulated a flyer notifying students of a mural project taking place on Saturday of that week.

When Saturday arrived, more than twenty students showed up to help. The English teacher came, too, and the school janitor, and the lady from the cafeteria, who brought tart, sweet lemonade and oatmeal cookies to share. Miss Riemer brought supplies, and before anyone began, she covered the wall with a fresh coat of white paint to give everyone a clean canvas on which to work. When most of the wall was covered in white, she pulled out her tiniest detail brush, and gently painted around the small flowers and creatures Mika had already created.

Then everyone else got to work. Brushes slapped the concrete and colors dribbled as the wall became filled with bright sun and blue sky, and the colorful plants and animals below it. There was an arbor, with wild pink roses twisted along its curve, and a little stone path. Blue birds flew overhead, and rich brown soil sparkled like coffee. A striped orange cat came to join the children, and one of them painted his likeness on the wall, curled up in the sun in a corner of the garden. Like the book they were reading in school -- The Secret Garden by Frances Hodgson Burnett -- this was becoming an enchanted place.

But this garden was not secret. While the children worked, an audience gathered. Among those people were the teenagers who had defaced the wall. They stood defiantly watching, waiting for the chance to step in, and to reclaim what they saw as their property.

One of the teenagers stepped forward, shaking a can of spray paint. The children fell silent. Only Mika moved. She dipped a brush into the can of red, and said to the boy, "Would you like to add a ladybug?"

The boy frowned, then looked down at his shoes. The air was quiet for a full minute. He put down the can of spray paint, and said, "Yeah. I can do that." His hand shook as he slowly and carefully put a circle of red on the daisy's leaf. Mika handed him a brush dipped in black, and said, "Here. For the spots." The boy rubbed his chin and stepped back. "No. You do it," he said. He glanced toward the far end of the wall. "I want to add a spider in the corner."

It was then that the other teenagers slowly came forward, and each one took a brush. One began painting grass, another, clouds. By the end of the day, every space on the wall was filled, and what was once ugly had become beautiful.

101

Miss Riemer squeezed Mika's hand, and rubbed at a smudge of blue paint on her cheek. "You did this," she said. Mika looked at all of the faces standing there and at the work they had done, together. She shrugged. "We all did." Her teacher kissed the top of her head. "Yes, we all did. But you were the seed."

No one ever painted graffiti on the wall again, and the very teenagers who had vandalized it became its guardians. And, Mika no longer held her breath when she walked by it. The wall was now a source of joy.

WENDY WOLF BIO

Wendy Wolf lives in the Seattle area (which she thinks is paradise) with her wonderful husband and beloved cats. She's been an artist for as long as she can remember, and a writer since not long after that (she had to learn the alphabet first). She's published poetry, essays, and illustrations, and has designed two book covers.

Wendy's favorite things (along with aforementioned husband and cats) are: books, food (especially mashed potatoes), friends, her brothers, sleeping in, being outside, long walks, animals, partly cloudy days, the ocean, and ice cold water (so cold you can hardly drink it). She's thrilled to have her stories included in this anthology, and hopes that they pass along to its readers some of the wonder and joy that books have given her. This is her first published work for children.

Alan And The Dream Stealer
Marie Twohey

"Oh, oh, we've gone too far. Time to go home,
Spot. Look where we are! That's Witches Hill and
you know what they say. It's scary, Spot. It's no
place to play. Bark all you want. I'm not throwing
that bone. I'm tired," said Alan. "I'm going
home." Then Spot grabbed his bone and ran up
the hill. He yelped once and then all was still.

"You come down here right now or there's no
treat tonight. Come back here," yelled Alan. Spot
was nowhere in sight. *Now what?* thought Alan, *I
want to go home, but Spot's my best friend. I can't
leave him alone.*

As he looked up the hill, it didn't look bad. The
bushes and trees seemed rather sad. When he
started to climb, though, he found soon enough,

103

there was more to that hill ---- weird, funky stuff. The bushes were moaning and hissed in his face. The rocks moved and chased him all over the place. The trees giggled and laughed when he started to slide. They were all around him. There was no place to hide.

As the rocks chased him, he slid in the dirt. He fell a few times, but he didn't get hurt. Trees were waving their branches. Leaves filled the air. He couldn't find Spot. He had looked everywhere.

He had about given up when he saw a bright light, in a strange little house almost hidden from sight. He tiptoed to it and knocked on the door. A voice said, "Come in. I'll make room for one more."

With a loud FFTHT the door opened wide and before he knew it, he was inside. The room seemed to grow as he stood there and stared. There was so much to see he forgot to be scared. A grandfather clock stood against the far wall. There was a harp and a honeycomb and that wasn't all. There were eight chairs, three tables, cabinets, books, and strange little things in crannies and nooks.

On a chair in the corner sat the old Witch. On her lap was a cat whose tail twitched and twitched. Next to the Witch, tied to her broom, was Spot, the most pitiful sight in the room.

"What brings you here, boy? Are you all alone?"

"Yes Ma'am. Come on Spot. It's time to go home."

"Oh, no," said the Witch. "You can't go, not yet. We'll have to have tea, after all, we just met."

"We have to go now. Mother's waiting for me."

"You can't go right now. First we'll have to have tea!"

"I don't want any tea. We want to go home."

"If you do," said the Witch, "then you'll go home alone. Quite often, I find things are not what they seem. You're not going home until you give me a dream!"

"A dream," Alan said, "why would you want that?"

"Oh, oh, that does it," hiccupped the black cat.

"I try to be nice. I try to be fair, but you're like all the rest. You really don't care. You know what I'll do if you're not nice to me? I'll turn you into a brown scrawny tree!"

"That may not be true, you know," whispered the cat. "Although she sounds mean, I don't think she'd do that. My name is Fernando," the big black cat said.

"Eli is mine," said the hat on her head. "Why don't you give her a dream that you've had? You don't know what happens when this Witch gets mad."

"I dream about baseball and football and stuff. She wouldn't want that. Football gets pretty rough."

"Well, I've offered," said Eli "She doesn't want mine. I dream about hat racks most of the time."

"That's right," said Fernando. "I dream about mice. How they run when I chase them. She says that's not nice."

"Hush up," hissed the Witch. "Hush up, you two. You know not to speak until you've been spoken to!"

"You've got one more quick chance to give me a dream. If you do then I'll give you some nice ice cream."

"I don't have any dreams that are right for a Witch."

The Witch was so mad, her ears started to twitch. "You do as I say or I'll fix you for good. You'll never get out of this dark, scary wood. I'll turn you into a yucky brown worm and I'll poke you and pinch you and laugh when you squirm!"

"I don't have one to tell you. You're not being fair. And turn me into a worm – why you wouldn't dare!"

"I'll do as I please, you mean, rude little boy. In fact, you would look good as a big windup toy." She pointed her broom and she zapped out a spell. That spell, thank goodness, did not go quite well. Alan ducked and the spell whizzed on by.

"Horsefeathers," said Grandfather Clock with a sigh. "Why doesn't she watch where she's pointing that thing? My springs are all bent from the last Zing, Zang, Zing!" And with that last Zing he turned into a bear with a ball on his nose and one foot in the air.

"Wow," yelled Fernando as he leaped on the hat. I'm so glad I didn't get caught up in that.

We're safe here, Eli, unless she points it straight up."

"Watch your claws, there, Fernando. Don't be so rough!"

Eli told Alan, "Hide behind that big chair. If you curl up real small, she won't know that you're there."

She was flying around, zapping this, zapping that. The cat bounced along on the top of her hat. Oh, she was mad. She was fit to be tied. There wasn't one spell that the Witch hadn't tried.

With everything changing the room got quite full, six turtles, eight toads and a very mad bull. Alan was creeping behind the big chair when he got a surprise – can you guess who was there?

"Ah, ha," said the Witch. "Now you'll not get away. This just might turn into a very nice day. You sit right where you are, and here, you can hold Spot. For such a small dog, he does whine a lot. This room may be big but it's not big enough. I think I had better get rid of this stuff."

As she flew around undoing each spell, she shouted to Alan, "you know perfectly well, that people dream every time they're asleep. That's all I want, just a dream I can keep. Once I had a dream and it had nice things in it. It didn't stay long, only lasted a minute."

"Oh," said Alan. "That couldn't be true. You said Witches don't dream, at least Witches like you."

"It is true, it is. Oh, you mean little boy. I was a princess with a frog for a toy." The Witch stopped in mid-air and she shut her mouth tight.

107

"You goofed," shouted Alan. "You sure goofed all right. You told me your dream. Now it's not yours anymore."

"Yeow," yelled the cat as they crashed to the floor.

The Witch on her knees was a sad blob of black. "Oh, please, please," the Witch cried, "won't you please give it back? It's only a small one, no more than a minute. There's even a bit of pure happiness in it."

Alan looked at the Witch, such a pitiful sight. "Oh, well," Alan said, "oh I guess it's not right." Her nose was so drippy. Her eyes were all red. Eli, her hat was scrunched down on her head. "I can't take your dreams, Witch. You've got it all wrong. And to tell you the truth, I knew all along."

"Your dreams they will always belong just to you. You are the one who can make them come true. Why, you can dream dreams without being asleep. Wide awake you can dream and have dreams you can keep."

"You mean, I, me, myself could have dreams just like you and I, me, myself, I could make them come true?"

"Yes," said Alan. "That's what life's all about. You are in charge of how your dreams work out."

"Oh," said the Witch, "I'm so glad you came. Things here will change. They will not stay the same."

"So, what's new about that," asked Eli the hat?

"You mean no more zapping?" asked Fernando the cat.

"Well," said the Witch, "a zap here, a zap there. Only once in awhile. I do try to be fair."

"Come on, Spot," said Alan. "We've a long way to go. It's still quite a walk down this dark hill, you know."

"Why walk," said the Witch, "when we can all fly." "I'll wait here," said old Grandfather Clock with a sigh.

So, they climbed on her broom and flew off down the hill. As far as I know, the Witch dreams her dreams still.

MARIE TWOHEY BIO

Marie Twohey is a member of the National Society of Children's Book Writers & Illustrators as well as a member of the Washington State Society of Children's Book Writers & Illustrators.

She lives in the Puget Sound area of Washington State with her family and enjoys writing to entertain her children and grandchildren, often using their delightful personalities as characters in her stories. The stories she enjoys the most are rhymed because she feels rhythm and rhyme play an important part in bringing out the precious parts of life and making the unpleasant ones easier to handle. She is an avid reader, hence her pen name Speeedreader.

Snow Soup And Blueberry Pie
GARY L. LARK

We used to have some snows around here. I'm telling you -- snow up to your belt buckle, snow up to your nose, snow up to no good. I remember one year it snowed a foot before I got my boots on. Two feet. Three feet. Cars disappeared. Horses and cows, if they weren't in the barn, were gone. I looked out of the dormer window upstairs; there was a lump of snow where the barn used to be. Kept snowing until it was plum over the rooftop.

One evening, I think it was evening, it's hard to tell when the sky is gone, we had a conference.

"We've got plenty of food in the larder to last a month or two," said Ma.

"Can we go out and play?" asked my brother Billy.

"We need to feed the cows, down at the barn," said Pa.

"Billy, you can't go out and play. We can't get out the door," said Ma.

"How are we going to get to the barn?" I asked. "Can we make a tunnel?" asked Billy.

"We'll have to tunnel our way out there, I suppose," said Pa.

"Oh, boy!" said Billy, running for his coat.

We all got our coats. Luckily, the shovels and wheelbarrow were on the back porch. We started digging into that wall of snow; but what could we do with the snow? "Put it in the guest room," said Ma.

So we wheelbarrowed the snow into the guest room. Load after load, we packed it in, closets first. In the meantime Ma put it to use: she made snow tea and coffee, snow Jell-O, snow jam, snow jelly, snow salsa, and started a big pot of snow soup.

We dug and we dug, packing the tunnel walls smooth. Ma brought out a lantern to light things up. It was a fine tunnel.

"Looks like we're going to have a lot of soup," said Ma, when we came in for lunch.

We tunneled all day and half the next.

"Shouldn't we be to the barn by now?" I asked. "We'll get there soon enough," said Pa.

So, we dug some more.

Now, back at the house Ma was making supper. I could smell the good smell of soup coming up the tunnel. Then it hit me: blueberry pie. Lord, nothing like blueberry pie in the middle of winter. That really got us going. We shoveled like crazy machines.

We were about ready to give it up for the night and head toward the blueberry pie when we struck a log. I'll be durned," said Pa. "Looks like we're off a little bit."

"What do you mean, 'off a little bit?'" I asked.

"We missed the barn, a little bit," said Pa.

"Oh," I said, thinking about them blueberry pies. About that time, we began to hear a strange noise, like a little motor, humming on the other side of the logs.

We got the sticks and limbs and logs cleared away and the little motor got louder. We held up the lantern and there was a bear! In a cave! That little motor was the bear snoring. We started to back out of the cave and cover it back up when the bear's nose began to twitch. It sniffed and sniffed, moving its sleepy head. While we were backing out the bear started to move toward us, still asleep.

We walked quiet and careful back to the house with that bear lumbering behind us. We shut the screen door on the porch when we got back, but the bear just hooked its claws around the edge and peeled it right off the hinges. Pa decided to leave the kitchen door open so he wouldn't have to fix it.

It was following its nose. I can't say I blame the bear any; the smell of blueberry pie is a powerful force.

Anyway, the bear clopped across the kitchen floor, still fast asleep, sniffing its way right to the table where two fine looking blueberry pies sat

113

cooling. My, they looked good. We all stood in a little circle, watching, as the bear sat down on the chair and stuck its nose in the middle of one of those pies, and began to slurp. When it was through with that one it switched to the other. We were all quiet. Even Billy knew better than to wake up a sleeping bear. It finished the second one, sniffed in the direction of the soup, burped, then climbed down from the chair and went back out the door.

We followed the bear up the tunnel and watched it shuffle back to bed. Pa and I shoveled snow back over the logs and sticks, packing it nice and tight.

That evening we had our soup and wished for blueberry pie.

"I'll make some more, there's still berries in the freezer," Ma said.

"I sure would like one of those pies right know," I said.

"I could eat two myself," said Billy.

"Maybe you should wait a day or two, Ma," said Pa. "We'll put a little more snow between the bear and the pies."

After we worked on the tunnel another day, Ma baked two of the grandest blueberry pies she ever made.

Oh, the cows? We studied the tunnel a bit and found where we zigged instead of zagged. The cows were a little hungry, but the barn had been cozy warm beneath the thick quilt of snow.

Come spring, when the snow was melted outside, we looked in that cave. The bear was

114

gone. I'll bet it had the sweetest blueberry pie dreams any bear ever had.

We used the last of the snow from the guest room to make snow cones for my birthday on the 14th of July.

Now that was some snow.

GARY L. LARK BIO

For the last thirty years, Gary Lark has worked as a librarian in public libraries. Ten years of that time was spent as children's librarian and storyteller. Gary has been a writer since high school, and when he became immersed in children's literature, he began writing stories for young people. He still reads extensively in that area.

Currently he is a part-time reference librarian at the Coos Bay Public Library. Before becoming a librarian, he worked as a hospital aide, carpenter, janitor, and salesman. Experience being the best writing instructor, Gary has had a broad education. He is also a graduate of Oregon State University.

Gary grew up along the bank of the Umpqua River in Oregon and spent many years fishing, swimming, and learning from its constant grace. Gary has edited the anthologies Luckiamute I and

II, published the chapbook Eels and Fishes, and has published widely in journals such as: North American Review, Story Quarterly, Crab Creek Review, Blue Unicorn and Adoption Therapist. His play, *And One Flew South*, won first place in the 2002 Pacific Northwest Writers Association literary contest.

Gary Lark's latest book of poems is *Tasting the River in the Salmon's Flesh*.

Editorial Note about the next story, ***The Good For Nothing Ghost*** – The author, Julyan Davis, writes with an excellent command of Appalachian dialect (A *haint* is dialectic for a *haunt* or a ghost.) and tradition. The story takes readers into this unique and timeless mountain place.

The Good For Nothing Ghost
Julyan Davis

Used to be the mountains were quiet enough for just about anyone to come up on a ghost or two. That's how mountain folk know a deal about ghosts and haints and the like. Such as first of all, a ghost starts off looking real as you or me before it gets to fading. Second of all, that you can be live and breathing and still have left your haint someplace. A haint is just a mark you leave by feeling a thing strong enough, and not just wretchedness, neither.

Take Nathan Martin's old blue tick hound-- folks still see the ghost of that old dog wagging his whole length and wailing with the sheer joy of going hunting one evening. Or young Grover Clay who got the courage to go courting Sally Pickett, a girl as pretty as a bee, only to come up on his own ghost, sharp as a picture, standing there with his mouth wide open on the very spot he first saw her.

All of which leads me to the story of the good for nothing ghost and my uncle Hoyt. A story that

117

proves a living feller can leave a ghost, clear as anything, and just because he's so caught up in himself. It also proves one thing wrong: that you can shift a ghost by fixing a haunted house with new timber.

My uncle Hoyt Stiles bought a cabin and some land that had a haint from the first day. My aunt Cora went up to speak to a boy in the yard and he just disappeared like that.

"Well," she told my uncle, "he's not a thing in the world but a ghost."

Uncle Hoyt went to see the man who sold him the cabin but he was long gone.

This ghost showed up all the time. Sometimes he'd be sitting on the porch, sometimes he'd by lying in the orchard, and sometimes he'd be gazing at the stove. Uncle Hoyt said at least the feller wasn't in the habit of startling a person with sudden movement. My aunt Cora said the boy was pining for a girl and they were buried together someplace. So they both felt mostly sorry for the haint and took to saying a kind word when they saw him.

Then one day came a knock at the door and there was the ghost talking at my uncle. Uncle Hoyt could hear him and he could smell him and when he saw how their visitor looked a little older, he figured it out.

"You left your haint here, son," he said. "We've been stepping over you these past three years."

"Lord have mercy," said Aunt Cora.

The man was real curious. "I got me a ghost?"

he said. His name was Grady Runion and he had grown up right where they were standing. Then he walked across the room and sat down by the stove like he had never left. It was nearly evening and he looked like a man hoping for supper. "You fixed the place up," he said.

"Your family build this place?" asked my uncle. "That was my pa," said Grady Runion, "but I helped with most everything."

Uncle Hoyt thought about the old roof leaking and the chimney that wouldn't draw and the sag in the floor and every useless door and window he had spent the last three years fixing and only just now finally finished but he said nothing. Aunt Cora gave their guest a plate of apple butter and biscuits and Grady Runion commenced to eat like he meant to kill himself that way.

"I'm just sorry for whatever wretchedness sprung a ghost out of you," said my aunt, kind of curious.

Then Grady Runion looked puzzled. "Don't reckon I had time for such," he said. "Why there wasn't a minute to the day a body could rest, chores were so thickety around." He looked sorry for himself. "I reckon I just felt tired."

My uncle thought about the ghost just sitting in the sun, and sleeping under the apple trees, and cluttering up the stove like he was right then and he opened the door.

"Mister," he said, "I've figured you out. You're a good for nothin' ghost and a good for nothin' man."

Grady Runion took the point like it was real

familiar, but something about my uncle just then persuaded Grady to make a kind of jump for the door and he didn't stop till he had run an extry mile.

My aunt Cora picked up the plate and then she said, "We'll put that haint to work." They left a broom for the ghost on the porch. They stood a ladder and basket where he lay in the orchard. They filled his place at the stove with a stack of wood.

"Git to sweeping, Grady Runion," Aunt Cora would say.

"Ain't that fire lit?" Uncle Hoyt would ask.

That was how they got the ghost of Grady Runion to fading. Even a ghost should have known not to try and fool a Stiles. Their haint got to be less and lesser'n that.

If you go up there now my aunt Cora will show you what's left of a good for nothin' ghost, looking for all the world like a little piece of mist left over from the morning.

Editorial Note: Stories for *Beyond Time and Place* were numbered for blind judging so it came as a surprise that four authors had each written two winning stories. In the case of Julyan Davis, it was even more surprising because of the great difference between the language, setting, theme, and tone of the two stories. With an attuned ear for dialect, Julyan Davis moves from the mountain speech of Appalachia to a more standard form of English in The Greatest Painting in the World.

For JULYAN H. DAVIS BIO, see next story

The Greatest Painting In The World
Julyan Davis

One day, long ago, a famous artist arrived at the place of his childhood. To reach his home he had traveled in a great circle. When he left, he was poor and unknown. Now, many years later, he was recognized wherever he went.

The whole town came out to welcome him, lining the streets and throwing flowers around. Once this had been all he wanted but now it meant nothing. His name was Bartholomew Brown and he had come back to paint the greatest picture in the world.

At the first of a dozen banquets in his honor, Bartholomew Brown stood up. "Thank you people of Bington," he said. "I have come back to paint the greatest picture in the world."

Everybody gasped. What would it be? A huge portrait of the mayor and his family? A fantastic painting of fruits and flowers with every detail, even a tiny fly, or a drop of water on the side of a plum? A lovely view with cows and sheep and big fat clouds? A poor sad clown beside the sea? Finally, someone asked the artist.

"That," shouted Bartholomew Brown, "is the surprise!"

Everyone cheered, though goodness knows why, because the whole town had been hoping for a great big painting of the town hall to go inside the town hall. Now they had no idea what they would get.

Bartholomew Brown's assistants prepared the studio for him. They lined the shelves with jars of paint. The pigment, like spoonfuls of brightly colored dust, was ground up with oil to make the paint. Some of the colors were very expensive. They were made from the rarest things: a purple from the tiniest part of a tiny seashell, a deep red ground up from real gems. There were brushes of every kind: huge flat brushes to paint all the blue in a sky, tiny pointed brushes to draw in the eyelashes of a greyhound. Then the studio was ready.

"How big do you think this painting is going to be, lads?" shouted Bartholomew Brown.

He shouted a lot. They shook their heads.

"Gigantic, boys," he smiled. "The biggest by far. Twenty times, you heard right, son, twenty times bigger than anything I've done!"

All the servants slapped each other on the back and grinned like wild men, though goodness knows why, because they were going to have to stretch the thing. Before you paint on a canvas, you have to stretch it over a wooden stretcher and nail it down good and tight on the back. They spent another week crawling all around and under and over the huge sheet and the huge beams of the stretcher. When that was done, they had to paint the whole canvas white, twice!

Then Bartholomew Brown ordered a huge picture frame to be made for the painting he had not even started.

"Think how long it will take to carve the frame," he explained. "It has to be at least three feet thick and I want all manner of twiddly little bits carved into it. Then they will have to cover it in gold. "

"It will weigh a ton," said one of the assistants. "At least!" laughed Bartholomew Brown. "Pity the poor wall that has to hold it up."

"And the poor nail," added another assistant.

When the morning came for the famous artist to start work, he did not know where to begin. The canvas was as big as the side of a house. It was so white his eyes were full of those strange, floating, wispy things you sometimes see on a bright day.

"It's a biggie," he told the mayor. "Oh, it's a big 'un all right." The mayor nodded and smiled, though goodness knows why, because anyone could see even then that Bartholomew Brown had bitten off more than he could chew.

Poor Bartholomew Brown. He went for a walk to clear his head. For the first time he wished he were a little less boastful. Now everybody expected great things from him. In fact, they expected the greatest painting in the world. The truth was he really preferred to paint little pictures. The truth was this huge painting frightened him. He walked round and round the park and even the pigeons seemed to guess his plight.

Weeks went by. Months went by. Though he had worked as hard as he could, every morning Bartholomew Brown rubbed out what he had painted the day before. He looked stranger and stranger. His hair grew long and his clothes needed changing. He had paint on his face and food on his shirt. What had he done so far? The famous artist would let nobody know, not even his assistants. He had put a huge curtain in front of the canvas and no one, absolutely no one, was allowed to look.

Many years went by. Bartholomew Brown had become a great mystery. What could have taken so long? Some people said he had run away. Behind the curtain, the painting looked very odd. It looked like twenty paintings all jumbled together. There were soldiers and horses and a dragon. The sun shone in one corner and the moon in another. There was a banquet table and a storm, chickens and a sailing ship.

Bartholomew Brown was just finishing a butterfly when the curtain shook.

"Mr. Brown?" quavered the mayor's voice. "Hello, Mr. Brown?" It was a very old voice now and the mayor a tiny shrunken old man. Then suddenly, to the artist's horror, the mayor crawled under the curtain.

"You can't come in here!" shouted Bartholomew Brown.

"I'm sorry, Mr. Brown," said the mayor, "but it's been twelve years and..." He stopped and stared.

Bartholomew Brown stopped shouting and watched the mayor. He swept the hair off his forehead, which left a long yellow streak of paint across his brow.

"Magnificent!" said the mayor, though goodness knows why, because it was certainly the craziest, busiest painting he had ever seen, impossible to hang anywhere or match to any sofa. Then he told Bartholomew Brown the bad news. The town had decided that twelve years was long enough. He was to get no more money until he had something ready for the town hall.

Bartholomew Brown screamed. Then he pulled down the curtain and tried to wrap himself in it but it was just too big and heavy. Still yelling, he turned over all his jars of paint and threw his brushes at the ceiling. Then he rolled around in all the mess until he was a hundred different colors. The assistants and the mayor just watched. Then Bartholomew Brown looked up and said quietly, "How big does this thing have to be?"

"Any size," the mayor said, crossly now, "Just finish it."

Bartholomew Brown lay on his back and looked at the painting for a long time. The dragon looked good. So did the basket of fruit. The chicken was one of his best.

"Gather round boys," he said. The assistants stood in a ring looking down at the brightly colored artist.

"Hugo, get the scissors, the big ones!" he shouted. "Finchley, get the straight edge! Bramwell, get the picture framer! We have work to do!" He leapt to his feet like a yellow and orange, gold and green firework.

The great day came for the town to see the painting. People came from miles around. Children had grown up hearing about the mystery artist behind the curtain, and now they brought their own children to see the masterpiece. The doors to the hall opened and the crowd swept inside.

What a sight met their eyes! There was not one, but twenty masterpieces! Round and round the people went, whispering their amazement.

"Did you see that dragon?" one asked. "What about the chicken?" said another.

Then Bartholomew Brown entered the room and everyone cheered. Flowers were thrown at him and they caught in his hair like a crown. Only the mayor knew that he had chopped one painting into twenty smaller ones, but he said nothing. Bartholomew Brown smiled. He was scrubbed and clean and happy for the first time in twelve years.

All those paintings hang in museums now, but hidden away in the great attic in Bington's town hall, behind one enormous dusty curtain, is an old picture frame. It has never been used, though goodness knows why, because it is possibly the greatest picture frame in the world: as long as a house, still bright gold, and covered with all manner of twiddly little bits.

JULYAN H. DAVIS BIO
Julyan Davis is originally from Bath, England. In 1988, having completed his art training at the Byam Shaw School of Art in London, he traveled to the American South. This trip was inspired by his interest in the history of Demopolis, Alabama and its settling by Bonapartist exiles in 1817. In Tuscaloosa, Julyan met his future wife, Madeleine, and he has resided in the South since.
In his career as a painter, he has focused on the American landscape. He is known for his paintings of the mountains of North Carolina and Deer Isle, Maine. He and Madeleine live in Scaly Mountain, North Carolina.

Artwork by Pam Veal Warner

A Super Socks Story
Lucy N. Adams

Sam and Suzee Socks were a happy pair. Every time their friend Bobby found them resting in his dresser drawer, he wanted to wear them. They were soft. Their gray and red stripes made them his favorite. His mom often said they didn't match what he was wearing that day, but Bobby always said, "Who cares?"

Sam and Suzee snuggled in Bobby's tennis shoes as he ran and jumped. When he pulled off his shoes, they were proud to show off their colors and very happy to be out of those smelly tennis shoes.

Those were the times when his mom held her nose and said, "Whew, Bobby, those socks smell to high heaven! Put them in the dirty clothes hamper." He wasn't sure what heaven had to do with his socks, but his mom didn't look very happy when she said it.

One night after Bobby took his bath, he searched in the clothes hamper for his favorite socks. Even though they were dirty, he put them on again and jumped into bed. Sam and Suzee were excited to sleep in a real bed, but while Bobby slept, his mom tiptoed into his room and took off his socks! Sam and Suzee were sad that they were thrown into the clothes hamper again.

There they rested until the next morning when Bobby's mom dumped all the dirty clothes into the washing machine. Each time they were washed, they always gurgled and said, "We don't like this. Get us out!" However, as the dirt washed away and Sam and Suzee were clean again, they felt great!

Next they tumbled around and around in the warm dryer. That was lots of fun! When all the clothes were dry, it was time to get out.

That's when the problem began. Somewhere between the dryer and the folding table, the socks got separated from one another. Sam lay there alone. "Suuuu-zeeee!" he shouted. "Suuuu-zeeee!"

There was nothing for him to do but lay there on the table. Tears trickled down his red stripes as he whimpered, "No one needs just one sock, what will happen to me?" As the days went by, he was pushed farther and farther back on the folding table.

One horrible day, Bobby's mom had the nerve to use Sam as a dust rag! She squirted him with lemon oil and swished him over the living room tables.

"Ugh," he coughed. "Stop it. I belong to Bobby."

Then one day as Bobby's mom swept between the washer and the dryer, something stuck to her broom. "Oh, there it is - the missing sock," she said.

Suzee's pretty red stripes were covered with dust, which caused her to sneeze.

After blowing the dust off of Suzee, Bobby's mom found Sam on the table and put the pair together. She folded them and placed them in Bobby's dresser drawer.

Sam and Suzee hugged and cuddled. They talked about the terrible days of loneliness when they thought they would never be together again. She had been calling for Sam but he never heard her.

The next morning as Bobby dressed to go out to play, he looked in his dresser drawer. He saw brown socks, red socks, and blue socks. Oh, how he wished he could find his favorite socks again. They had been missing a long, long time but then, guess what he found?

Sam and Suzee were tucked in between those other socks. They kept calling to Bobby, "Hey look over here, we're back again."

Even though he didn't hear them - he found them!

How proud they were as he shouted to his mom, "Hey Mom, I found my favorite socks again."

They giggled as he pulled them onto his feet. Sam and Suzee were excited to be running and jumping again with Bobby.

They were even happy to snuggle into those smelly old tennis shoes!

LUCY N. ADAMS BIO

Lucy Neeley Adams is a singer, songwriter, and storyteller who lives in the mountains of Lake Junaluska, North Carolina. The wife of a United Methodist minister, they have served together in ministry for over forty years.

In 1984, Lucy created the radio program *The Story Behind the Song* aired on Christian radio station WWGM in Nashville, Tennessee. The five-minute show answered the questions "Why do people write songs?" and the who, what, where and why of the hymn. The stories behind the hymns grew into articles for numerous publications. Her book *52 Hymn Story Devotions* was published by Abingdon Press in 2000. In 1998, Lucy Adams was chosen 'Writer of the Year' by the Cookeville Creative Writers.

Jefferson Oscar Edison
(Better Known As Joe) And The New Girl
Alice M. Shourds

Jefferson Oscar Edison
(better known as Joe)
was the sneakiest, meanest bully
you'd ever care to know.

He never laughed or smiled,
he gave you nasty looks.
He bumped into you every day
and made you drop your books.

Whenever he sat behind you
he always pulled your hair.
He made up rules for every game
but never played them fair.

Each morning when he rode the bus
he'd hog most of the seat.
When we stood quietly in the hall
he'd stomp on all our feet.

At lunch he smacked when he chewed his food,
he left garbage everywhere.
He burped real loud right in your face
and didn't even care.

Yes, Jefferson Oscar Edison
(better known as Joe)
was the sneakiest, meanest bully
you'd ever care to know.

He threw dirt on all the playground slides,
he tangled all the swings.
He mixed the paints in art class,
in music he'd yell instead of sing.

He tied our jump ropes into knots,
let air out of basketballs.
One day he even roller-skated
through the school house halls.

He colored on the classroom desks,
he broke most all the toys.
He spilled the glitter and the glue
then blamed other girls and boys.

Yes, Jefferson Oscar Edison
(better known as Joe)
was the sneakiest, meanest bully
you'd ever care to know.

One morning I'd decided
that's it, enough's enough.
It was time to let that bully know
he was really not that tough.

The bus pulled up and I got on,
prepared to sit with Joe,
but sitting right beside him was
a girl I didn't know.

So I took the seat across from them
and stared for quite awhile,
"til something really strange took place,
mean Joe began to smile.

He'd slid over in that seat today,
he'd straightened up his hair.
And when we got into the class
he saved that girl a chair.

At recess mean Joe asked real nice
to join us in our games.
He followed rules and when he lost
he didn't call us names.

Joe lined up quietly at lunchtime,
he didn't stomp our feet.
He used good manners when he chewed,
we could hardly hear him eat.

All that day Joe sat and smiled,
he never gave us nasty looks,
and walking out to catch the bus
he carried that new girl's books.

Yes, Francis Latisha O'Grady
(better known as Flo)
did all of us a favor that morning
when she sat down next to Joe.

Because Jefferson Oscar Edison
(better known as Joe)
changed his ways from mean to nice
all because of Flo.

Editorial Note: Stories for *Beyond Time and Place* were numbered for blind judging so it came as a surprise that four authors had each written two winning stories
For ALICE M. SHOURDS BIO see next story

Special Delivery
Alice M. Shourds

Under my bed lives a creature.
I hear it every night.
Mommy and Daddy don't believe me,
my big brother says "yeah, right."
But I know it's there each evening
when I crawl into bed,
so I pull the blanket tight
and put the pillow over my head!
Still I can hear it moving,
scratching and clawing the floor.
If I weren't so scared I'd jump out of bed
and run right out the door.
Instead, I lie there wondering
how long the creature plans to stay.

I wonder, too, just what does he do
stuck here in my room all day?
It probably plays with my toys
while I'm away at school...
suddenly I thought of the perfect plan,
I knew what I had to do.

There was no school tomorrow,
I'd pretend to sleep really late.
I'd stay in my bed, very quiet,
I'd wait and wait and wait.
Next morning I waited for that creature
to crawl out from under my bed.
Then, quickly, I tossed my big blanket
over the top of it's big, hairy head.
I tied it up tight with my jump rope,
threw it into a big, cardboard box,
and to keep it from biting and yelling,
I stuffed its mouth with my socks!
I hurried and stapled the box shut,
then wrapped all around it with tape.
No way would that strange, scary creature
ever, ever escape.
I took out my case of markers,
and using the really dark blue,
I wrote in great big letters
SPECIAL DELIVERY, TO THE ZOO!
Carefully I carried the box downstairs,
in each corner I stuck on a stamp,
lucky for me Mom keeps them
on top of the desk by the lamp.
I hurried off to the post office,
down the sidewalk that box I was draggin'.

Boy, was I glad it wasn't too big
to fit in my little, red wagon.
At the post office, I left the box sitting
outside, up against the front door.
As I hurried back home, I said to myself
"no more creature, HURRAY, no more!"

That very same night something happened
when I was all tucked into bed.
I heard a loud bump, that made me jump,
then a rather strange something said...
"WHERE'S MY BABY"?
I was too scared to move, I just couldn't believe
there could possibly be another.
But standing there drooling at the side of my bed
was that creatures' really mad mother!
I took a deep breath as I calmed myself down
'cause I knew what I had to do.
Yes, early next morning, you guessed it,
she was on her way to the zoo!

Now with both of those creatures gone
you would think I'd be really glad.
Do you want to know why I'm not?
Tonight... I met the Dad!!

HERE WE GO AGAIN!

ALICE M. SHOURDS BIO
Alice M. Shourds was born in Redfield, South
Dakota and now lives in Kissimmee, Florida
where she is a teacher's assistant at Pleasant Hill

Elementary School.

She is married, has 4 children and 4 grandchildren, and has enjoyed writing stories for all of them as well as illustrating most of the stories. The greatest sources of her ideas are her own children and experiences at work.

She also enjoys writing poetry and had one published in an anthology of poems. In addition to writing, other pleasures are woodworking, drawing and spending as much time as possible with her family.

Artwork by Todd Ballantine

Iggity Biggity Oogity Snizzard
Olina St. Onge

Tam Boo was once a very great wizard. He could make the mountains grow bigger and people grow smaller. He could turn a horse into a lion or a mouse into a man. People far and wide feared Tam Boo.

However, that was long ago.

Now Tam Boo is a very old wizard. He can't remember most of the spells to turn people into animals or trees into tigers. What he **can** remember is how to make a blizzard. That is his favorite thing. Sometimes though, he even forgets how to make a blizzard.

"Now let me see. Is it iggity biggity oogity fizzard or iggity biggity oogity mizzard?" he mumbles to himself. "Oh well, I'll try IGGITY BIGGITY OOGITY SLIZZARD, MAKE

BEFORE ME NOW A BLIZZARD!" He waves his magic wand and instead of a blizzard, he creates dozens of lizards.

Tam Boo is not one to give up. He keeps trying even though he might end up with a herd of lizards or a room full of confused wizards. Eventually he'll get it right and have a fantastic blizzard. Then Tam Boo will sit in his favorite chair and listen to the wind howl. He'll smile and hug himself tightly as he watches the billion snowflakes swirl around his little house.

The people in Tam Boo's little town are not so fond of the wizard's blizzards. They have begged him, "Please, stop making those blustery snow storms." It is difficult for the farmers to grow their vegetables when the ground is covered in snow. You can just imagine how long it takes clothes to dry when there are twelve-inch icicles hanging from sleeves, and is it ever shocking to be swimming in a warm pond one minute and nearly frozen in ice the next!

Tam Boo has tried very hard not to create blizzards. He took up bowling to get his mind off howling winds and swirling snowflakes, but when the bowling ball struck the pins, the sound gave him such a start he shouted, "IGGITY BIGGITY OOGITY SNIZZARD, MAKE BEFORE ME NOW A BLIZZARD!" and a tremendous blizzard began to blow.

Tam Boo felt very badly even though it was one of the greatest blizzards he had ever created.

He decided to join the Scrabble Club. Surely, this would keep his mind off blizzards.

142

That worked or a little while. But when Tam Boo was able to make fifty seven points by spelling the word snowstorm on a red square, he was so thrilled he cried, "IGGITY BIGGITY OOGITY SNIZZARD, MAKE BEFORE ME NOW A BLIZZARD!" and what do you know. Outside the winds began blowing and snow swirling. For a few minutes Tam Boo was so excited he forgot his promise to the townspeople. He ran to the window to watch the twirling snowflakes and hugged himself tightly.

When he turned to his fellow scrabble players they were scowling. Once again, Tam Boo felt badly. He hung his head and mumbled, "Sorry."

Now what could Tam Boo do to take his mind off snowstorms? He thought and thought. "Knitting! That's what I can do." So Tam Boo joined the knitting club in the town hall.

Old Mrs. Crabbit was the best knitter in town and she agreed to teach Tam Boo. Many days went by without a blizzard. The townspeople were so happy. The vegetables began to grow, the clothes dried in the hot sun, and the children swam in the warm pond.

Mrs. Crabbit taught Tam Boo many different patterns like the sun stitch, the star hook, and the scoop-the-loop. Tam Boo really liked the scoop-the-loop. Then Mrs. Crabbit taught Tam Boo the snowflake stitch. That did it. Tam Boo couldn't help himself. He sat on his hands, he stuffed a ball of yarn in his mouth, he put a pillow over his head, but nothing could stop him. "IGGITY BIGGITY OOGITY SNIZZARD, MAKE

BEFORE ME NOW A BLIZZARD!" he yelled. The winds began to howl, the door slammed, snowflakes blew in the open windows. Tam Boo felt so ashamed. He slowly left the room and walked home to his little house in the swirling snow.

That evening the townspeople met to discuss the fate of the wizard and his blizzards. "I'm afraid we're going to have to ask him to leave," said the mayor.

"It can't be helped," said the farmers. "It's for the good of the town," said the sheriff. The people were very sad. They really liked Tam Boo.

Just then, the door flew open and in ran Johnny the shepherd boy. "The Bald Bandits with the Blue Bandannas are coming. They're riding over the hill!" he cried.

"Not the Bald Bandits with the Blue Bandannas! They're the meanest, toughest bandits around. What are we going to do?" asked the mayor who was shaking in his boots. The townspeople huddled closer. They were so frightened.

Then Mrs. Crabbit had a great idea. "The wizard! Tam Boo can make the coldest blizzard yet and freeze the bald bandits!"

Everyone thought this was a fantastic idea and ran to the wizard's house to request his help. There they found a very sad Tam Boo packing up all his belongings. "Please don't go," said Mrs. Crabbit.

"We need you," said the mayor. "The Bald Bandits with the Blue Bandannas are coming. Please, Tam Boo, won't you make the biggest coldest blizzard ever? You can freeze the Bald Bandits!"

Tam Boo could hardly believe his ears. The townspeople were asking him, no begging him, to make a blizzard! "Do you really mean it?" he asked. The townspeople nodded.

"Well, of course I will. I'll make the fiercest blizzard you've ever seen!" Everybody took a step back and stood close together.

Tam Boo pushed up his glasses, rolled up his sleeves, and cleared his throat. In the loudest voice he could muster he yelled, "IGGITY BIGGITY OOGITY SLIZZARD, MAKE BEFORE ME NOW A BLIZZARD!"

Instead of a blizzard, dozens of lizards filled the room. The people began screaming as the lizards crawled over their shoes.

Tam Boo was so embarrassed! He waved his wand and the lizards disappeared.

He tried again. "IGGITY BIGGITY OOGITY GLIZZARD, MAKE BEFORE ME NOW A BLIZZARD!" he yelled as he waved his wand.

Suddenly there were two dozen very confused wizards scratching their chins and mumbling, "How'd I get here?"

"Oh my," mumbled Tam Boo as he ran his hand through his long white beard. "Please excuse an old, nervous wizard," he said to the other wizards and he waved his wand and they, too, disappeared. "Please, hurry Mr. Tam Boo. The Bald Bandits are getting closer," said Johnny the shepherd boy with his ear to the ground."

"Of course, of course," said Tam Boo as he

wrung his hands together. "I think I've got it. IGGITY BIGGITY OOGITY SNIZZARD, MAKE BEFORE ME NOW A BLIZZARD!"

The wildest wind began to blow. The walls began to creak. Snow blew through the open windows and a horrible howling was heard. The townspeople cheered. Tam Boo blushed mightily then ran to the window to admire his wonderful, fierce storm.

And what a storm it was! It blew and blew. After three tries and a couple of charred walls, Tam Boo created a fire to help the people stay warm. After some time, the winds began to die down. The sun peaked behind a cloud and shone on the little town and the snowflakes melted slowly as they drifted towards the ground.

The shepherd boy took the sheriff and several of the strongest people to the hill. There they saw a very strange sight. Ten bald bandits were frozen on their horses just as they were when the blizzard began. The sheriff and his crew quickly tied up the bald bandits before they could thaw. Then they built a fire and watched the snow and ice melt from the bald bandit's shiny heads.

Tam Boo became a hero that day. The townspeople decided he could stay and Tam Boo agreed to try to make just one little itty-bitty wizard blizzard a week. And in the wintertime, he could make the wildest, the fiercest wizard blizzard of them all.

OLINA ST. ONGE BIO

Olina St. Onge began writing children's books about ten years ago while taking a much-needed break from medical social work. Iggity Biggity Oogity Snizzard was one of her first children's story books written and was chosen for the writing contest because of its whimsical, silly nature. She is just a smidgen away from completing her second children's fantasy novel.

Writing children's books is not only a pathway for creativity for Olina, but also provides a fantastical escape from the challenges of the world. Olina lives in Southern Oregon with her beloved husband, Peter, their irresistible dog, Chanti, five endearing, elderly kitties, and seven serene koi fish. Her friend and daughter, Natalie, lives forever away in Portland, Oregon.

Olina is an animal rights activist and holds close to her heart a hopeful vision of compassion and peace for all beings.

I Have Two Dogs
Bobbi B. Ostrum

I have two dogs. Kouhoutek and Inky. Kouhoutek, you say it Ka-hooo-tek– my older brother named him after a comet. Kouhoutek is a black dog with tan eyebrows and white feet. His face is painted tan and white and he looks like a laughing clown. I've had him since I was two and now I'm ten. He's sneaky and smart and Dad calls him a "wise old dog." Inky is a big black dog with little brown eyes and lots of energy. She's a simple doggie – she likes to play and run and fetch tennis balls. She's younger, maybe 4 years old.

I play ball with Inky and Kouhoutek. Inky fetches the ball and Kouhoutek steals it from her. He used to fetch, but Inky is faster than him. Now he plays keep away instead. They like to chase me around the house and the pool, but Kouhoutek can't turn the corners as fast now. "He has hip problems," Mom says. "He's getting old." That makes me sad. I'd miss him if he died. So I give him and Inky lots of attention: brushing everyday and special treats and a nice new soft bed to sleep in. Kouhoutek and Inky sleep together every night. She would miss him too.

Today Kouhoutek is sick and Mom took him to the Veterinarian. Kouhoutek didn't come home. "The vet couldn't help him. It's for the best," my mom says. "He won't suffer anymore," my dad says. "He won't be in pain anymore," my parents say. But I miss him. I miss his fur and his eyes and his bark. I miss his tail wagging and hitting the ground when he sees me come home from school. I miss him stealing the ball when I throw it to Inky. I feel horrible. I don't want to eat. I don't want to play. I just want to cry and be alone. Inky doesn't understand Kouhoutek died. She howls and scratches at the door. She won't eat her food. She won't play. She's sad. She misses Kouhoutek too.

Inky is lonely in her bed, so I tuck her in tonight. I sit on her bed and pet her head and hold her paws. I whisper stories to her about Kouhoutek. "He could chase me around the pool and jump over the diving board. He could catch me every time. He could chase me around the house, but if I got too far ahead of him he would turn around to run the other way and surprise me. He was smart about that. He liked to chase my remote control cars and pick them up in his mouth. He came with my dad and me to fly my Baby Bat Kite and he let me hug him and cry when it crashed and broke. He would lick my face when I cried. He would bark and jump when I laughed. He had a long life and a good life. You will feel better soon. It's ok to be sad. We will be ok."

Inky falls asleep with my tears on her fur. I pet her head and then I go to bed too. My mom comes to tuck me in and holds my hand and strokes my hair and tells me "you will feel better soon. It's ok to be sad. We will be ok." She stays until I fall asleep.

Each night Inky comes to find me at bedtime and I sit with her again. I hold her paws and pet her head and tell her stories about Kouhoutek. She whines if I leave before she is asleep and most nights I cry at my memories. I miss Kouhoutek, but Inky needs me and I need her. We will feel better soon. We will be ok. Night after night we repeat our routine – I whisper stories to her, pet her head, and hold her paws. I remember all my favorite times with Kouhoutek and tell them to Inky.

Tonight my memories are happier and I laugh. Inky wags her tail and licks my face. Tonight I didn't cry and Inky went to sleep faster.

Tonight Inky didn't come looking for me to tuck her into bed. I check her bed and she is fast asleep. I scratch her ears and she opens one eye, wags her tail and it hits the floor, thump thump. I hug her and go to bed.

We still miss Kouhoutek, but we will be ok.

BOBBI B. OSTRUM BIO

Bobbi Ostrum grew up in California and developed her love of animals at an early age. Her family pets included dogs, cats, rats, guinea pigs, ducks, fish, and one hermit crab.

She has a Bachelor of Arts Degree in Communications from the University of Washington. Bobbi currently lives in Seattle with her husband, son, and two cats. This is her first published story.

Sassouma And The Clever Rabbit
Emily Rider-Longmaid

Once upon a time, when humans and animals still lived in peace and harmony with one another, there was a village in the southwest part of the beautiful country of Africa. This village had a calm river running through it and was surrounded by a peaceful, quiet forest. People and animals lived together in clay and mud hut houses with palm-leaf roofs. This village was an amazing place to live with its peacefulness and joy, until a man named Sassouma decided to make his home there.

Sassouma was disliked by almost everyone for his extremely narcissistic and selfish ways. Every day Sassouma went down to the river to bathe and then stare at his reflection for hours on end. After that, he would go home and count and recount all his gold, jewels, and valuables. Knowing how rich and beautiful he was, he would go into the village and brag about himself to whomever was willing to lend an ear. Animals and people did their best to ignore him, but Sassouma was a very persistent man.

"Hello my good man!" he would say to whomever would listen, "I can see you are looking at my fair figure. Wonderful, isn't it? Yes, I have worked hard for this appearance, but it is worth it, I must say." And on and on he would go, every day making himself seem even better, until the animals decided something had to be done. So, on a night when the air was heavy and damp with the smell of fresh vegetation, the grass was wet with dew, and the full moon shone bright with the twinkle of stars, the animals held their meeting.

"Welcome everyone," the king of the beasts started the meeting with his powerful voice, "I understand there is a problem with a certain person named Sassouma. People and animals alike have come to complain to me about his vanity and selfishness, and I understand something needs to be done. Does any one have any suggestions for what we might do with this man?"

"I do!" yelled the impulsive monkey whose loud cry could be heard throughout the kingdom. "Why don't we set up a trap? We could tell Sassouma that there's a fire and his wife was inside. Surely, he will rush in to save her. The fire will either severely scar him or even kill him."

"Good thinking," Lion replied, "yet we shall not jeopardize his life. He would know the risk of scarring and death, and he probably wouldn't dare to go into the fire. Does anyone else have an idea?"

"Well," said the hippo, who was known to sit and relax under the sun's great warmth in his river, "we could paint his face with dyes and creams when he's sleeping. When he goes down to the river to look at his reflection he will see an ugly face staring back at him, so he will become really scared and maybe even less narcissistic."

"You do have a good idea, however when Sassouma goes to bathe, the creams and paints shall wash off," responded Lion. " Does anyone have another suggestion?"

"Sort of," cawed the cuckoo who was known to be, well, cuckoo. "It's still developing, but since no one has any better plan, we could always have hippo sit on and squash Sassouma."

"Yes, I do believe that the idea is still developing," answered Lion, "and, if you remember, we do not want to kill the poor man. Anymore ideas?"

On and on this ordeal continued until it became almost a ritual of wild ideas being told by inventive animals. As the meeting went on through the night and into dawn where the sun peeped up over the mountains to welcome a sleeping village into a new day, the plans for the reformation of Sassouma become increasingly more ridiculous. Such animals as Snake, Cheetah, Gorilla, Weasel, and even Kangaroo shared thoughts and ideas.

"My friends," Lion interrupted the meeting, "we are all getting tired, and we are all offering silly ideas. We can start with another meeting tomorrow, but unless anyone objects, I am now going to stop this meeting and dismiss everyone."

"Wait!" a tentative cry from a bundle of soft, white fur; the clever and patient Rabbit was heard. "I have an idea that might work!" Slowly, Rabbit whispered his ingenious idea to the eager animals.

****

Two days later, when Sassouma went down to the river to bathe, he was extremely frightened by what he saw in his reflection. Instead of his usual reflection staring back him when he peered into the river, he saw a man with the skin of a zebra! Panicked, he rushed back to the village to find the Elephant, the wisest creature.

"Oh, Elephant, help me! How shall I get my regular skin back? What should I do?"

"Calm down Sassouma." Elephant replied quietly, "You shall have to do a couple of things to get this skin coloration off. If you do not do these things within three days, you will stay like this forever."

Hearing these words, Sassouma became alarmed and listened closely to what Elephant had to say. "First," Elephant instructed, "you must give half of your riches and valuables to the needy."

"Oh Elephant, please, no! Isn't there anything else I can do?" Sassouma pleaded.

"Unless you want to keep your form forever, no. Listen, and do not speak a word until I am done. Now, secondly, you must never brag or talk or show off your looks again. In addition, you must learn humiliation. If you do these things in three days, you will turn back to your old self. Now go and do as I say."

Not daring to say anything but thank you, Sassouma hurried off to do as directed. First, Sassouma gave up over half of his riches to the tribe's chief, trusting him to give them out fairly. Second, he promised the religious leader that he would never again be narcissistic or selfish. Finally, Sassouma went to all the people and animals to apologize for his nasty, selfish behavior. In three days time, Sassouma, to his happiness, was back to normal, or at least his normal looks. Once again, the village became happy and peaceful.

Later, Sassouma found out that the animals had a meeting and that Rabbit was the one who came up with the plan. The plan was for Mouse to sneak into Sassouma's house and pour an ancient potion into Sassouma's drink. However, the "zebra skin" that Sassouma acquired was not harmful, and Sassouma's regular skin would have returned even without Sassouma doing anything. Yet Sassouma was still grateful for the change, for he realized how important it is to not be vain or selfish.

EMILY RIDER–LONGMAID BIO
Emily Rider–Longmaid, lives in Massachusetts with her parents and brother. She wrote "Sassouma and the Clever Rabbit" when she was 12

years old. Emily likes to write and has had several short stories and a poem accepted for publication.

Emily has won academic awards, and is an avid soccer and basketball player. She loves science, Spanish, and spending time with friends.

Peggy And The Thief
Anne C. Kelley

Peggy preened her yellow and green feathers happily. What a glorious day! The bright sun reflected off the crystal ornaments on Mrs. Morgan's TV and broke into miniature rainbows on the floor. A spring breeze tugged at the frilly white curtains and filled the room with the scent of lilacs. Peggy flapped her wings and bounced on her swing. "What a fine day for flying," she squawked.

"I wouldn't if I were you," meowed Sam, a sleek Siamese cat lying on the floor under her cage. "Remember what happened the last time!" He yawned and curled up in the warm sunlight.

Peggy sighed. Sam was right. The last time she had practiced her rolls she had knocked over a priceless antique vase that Mrs. Morgan had inherited from her great-great-grandmother. The time before that she had upset a bottle of ink all over the letter that Mrs. Morgan was writing to her cousin. And the time before that... Peggy sighed. It was such a fine day for flying!

Peggy swung sadly on her swing and tried to think of something besides flying but it was no good. She just had to stretch her wings!

I'll be careful, she promised herself as she soared into the air. She flew slowly back and forth across the room, and then carefully rolled over. Oh, it felt good to be flying! She dove towards the floor, pulled up, and rose to the ceiling. Soon she was somersaulting across the room, diving and twirling gleefully.

She pulled out of a spectacular roll and glided in for a landing on Mrs. Morgan's polished table-top. CRASH! She collided with a lamp and it went tumbling to the floor. Peggy stared at it in disbelief. "Oh no," she cried, "not again!"

Sam opened one eye. "I told you so," he me-owed disdainfully. "You're so clumsy. I don't know why Mrs. Morgan puts up with you." His eye closed.

Peggy's feathers drooped, and large tears ran down her face. He's right again, she thought miserably. I am clumsy, probably the clumsiest parrot in the world. I try to be careful. I really do. Some-how, something always ends up broken or spilt or...still sobbing quietly she tucked her head under her wing and soon fell asleep.

The door of the apartment opened with a soft click. A thin, short man slipped inside. Closing the door behind him, he tiptoed over to Mrs. Morgan's desk and began to rummage through the drawers. He dug through the cupboards and looked under the couch. Finally, he grabbed some loose bills from Mrs. Morgan's old purse and shoved them in his pocket. He turned around and started to tiptoe back to the door.

Peggy sighed softly in her sleep. The stranger froze, one foot dangling in the air. Ever so slowly, he turned his head to look at the parrot. Satisfied that she was still sleeping, he lowered his foot.

"RAROOOUUW!" Sam leapt into the air, his injured tail arched above his back. He landed claws first on the thin man's shoulder. The thief screeched in pain. He grabbed Sam and threw him against the wall. Sam hit with a thud and lay still.

Peggy's eyes flew open and she squawked in alarm. The robber lunged for the door. His feet tangled in the cord of the broken lamp and he fell with a thump. Peggy swooped down on him, squawking and pecking at him with her strong beak. The thief cried out in anger and struggled to his feet. Grabbing an umbrella from the stand by the door, he swung it at Peggy. She ducked and he knocked the umbrella stand clattering to the floor. Peggy dove again, but the thief dodged and she crashed heavily into the TV. She lay on the floor beside Sam, trembling with fear.

The thief snickered. "Now I've got you," he sneered. He grabbed the frightened parrot. Peggy struggled feebly, but his grip was too strong for her to break. Her heart pounded in terror.

Just then, the door burst open and a police officer rushed in, closely followed by Mrs. Morgan. The robber loosened his hold on Peggy and she flew to the safety of her cage. The police officer handcuffed the man and led him to the door.

"It's a good thing that your neighbor heard all

the noise," the police officer said. He glanced at Peggy. "That's some parrot you've got there!"

Mrs. Morgan looked at the broken lamp and the scattered umbrellas. "Yes, it certainly is!"

Sam opened his eyes and stood up shakily. He slowly shook his head. "What...what happened?" he meowed. "Where am I?" Mrs. Morgan and the police officer laughed. Peggy laughed too. She happily preened her yellow and green feathers.

What a glorious day it had been!

ANNE C. KELLEY BIO

Anne Kelly is a teacher, a mother of four, and a writer from Dartmouth, Nova Scotia, Canada.

Anne graduated with a Bachelor of Child Study degree from Mount St. Vincent University in Halifax, and spent seven years teaching in northern Canada. She completed her Masters of Education in Teaching English as a Second Language, and has spent the last eleven years teaching ESL to adult immigrants. She presently coordinates a program which provides ESL instruction in the rural areas of Nova Scotia.

In 2000, Anne co-authored "Adjusting our Sails: Working With Immigrant Children in Today's Changing Communities," a project funded by the Department of Canadian Heritage. In 2001, she won the Joyce Barkhouse Writing for Children award from the Writers' Federation of Nova Scotia. She is currently working on her second Young Adult novel.

Shicksus
Len Silverman

Greg is like most boys in every way. He loves to play with his friends...pet his dog, Buster and giggle with his younger brother Ben. Greg's mother and father are like most parents. They read to Greg and Ben and share lots of love with them, too. Greg's house, though, is not like most people's houses, you see. It has a special person living in it...well, really, under it.

Greg met this strange man one day when his parents were giving Buster a bath in the back yard. As the dog splashed about and shook off the soapy water, Greg heard a very small, gravelly but very loud voice say "Are you trying to wash me out of my house, boy?"

Curious, Greg looked everywhere for the owner of that voice, but saw no one. He asked his parents if they heard it, but they had not. Only his little brother Ben seemed to have heard anything, but he didn't know where it came from either.

Suddenly, they heard it again. "Aren't you listening, boy?" Then they heard a sharp whistle from down near their feet. When they looked down, Greg and Ben saw the tiniest man they could have ever imagined. He was wearing green robes with red trim that went down to his feet. He also wore a tall red and green striped hat with a red ball on top. *He looks like an ice cream cone*, Greg thought. And he was so small. He was no bigger than Greg's hand. Greg knew that for sure because he had put his hand against the man's body to measure.

"Hey, keep your hands to yourself, do I look like one of your stuffed animals, boy? Let me tell you..." Before he could finish the sentence, Buster ran up, dripping with soapy water, and began to lick the little stranger. "Hey, knock it off! No... Nooo... Nooooo." His cries of anger, though, quickly turned into a fit of laughter as the little man began to stroke Buster's nose. "That'll do...that'll do," he said when he could finally catch his breath.

"Who are you," Greg suddenly asked. "What did you mean when you said 'my house'?" The little man laughed again.

"I suppose an introduction is in order...my name is Shicksus. My house is under your house...see?" Shicksus pointed to a tiny opening near the place where they stood. It looked so small that even a neighborhood mouse might pass it by without seeing.

"I live here and, well, look after things. It's my job." He shared a wide grin with Greg and Ben as he was now enjoying their little talk.

"Why couldn't my parents see you or hear you just then?" Greg asked.

"It takes a special kind of ears to hear me and a special kinds of eyes to see," Shicksus explained. "Kids have both special ears and special eyes ... parents don't." Buster then let out a low whimper. "Oh I forgot," Shicksus added, "dogs have 'em too!"

"Listen boys I need your help. That's why I came to you today, but you will have to see the problem for yourselves. Will you come with me?" Shicksus asked, motioning to the opening in the side of the house.

"How?" the boys said together, staring at the small hole trying to imagine what part of their bodies could possibly fit in such a small space. Greg finally said, "I couldn't even get my hand all the way in a hole that small!"

Shicksus only laughed. "Oh, did I forget to tell you boys that I know a bit of magic? Nothing fancy, but it's enough." With that, Shicksus removed a very tiny leather pouch from his robes. In the pouch was a sparkling gold power. He took a small pinch and blew a bit on each of the boys.

They looked at each other for a minute and then smiled. They knew all along that there is no such thing as magic, but before they could finish the thought, they both had the sudden urge to sneeze. "Ah…ahhh….aahhhhhh!", but the feeling passed. They both smiled. And then without warning it came. "AHHHHHHCHOOOOOOOO!"

The sneeze was so strong that each boy began spinning like a top. Faster and faster they spun. As they spun they began to get smaller. Spinning and shrinking, shrinking and spinning, until finally they were both the same size as Shicksus. *No, actually, they were a bit smaller*, Greg thought.

As if hearing Greg's thought out loud, Shicksus replied, "Well, what do you expect? I am a bit older than you two, you know." They all giggled.

Then, with a wink of his eye and a wave of his hand, Shicksus welcomed Greg and Ben to his home. As the boys stepped inside they were surprised to see a very cozy little house. The living room was filled with over-stuffed chairs and sofas with many pillows. From the tiny kitchen came the sweet aroma of

"COOKIES!", Ben shouted.

"Maybe we'll have one when our work is done," Shicksus said. "But for now, follow me."

As they journeyed deeper into the house, they began to notice something different. It wasn't as warm and cozy back here. When they finally entered Shicksus' bedroom they knew why. The floor was completely covered in water. There was water up to their knees. The tiny bed was floating like a small fishing boat and the television was filled with water like an aquarium.

"This is awful," Greg shouted. "But how can we help? We're just two little kids." As the boys listened with interest, Shicksus explained his plan to them. Once they heard what he had in mind, they agreed immediately and told him they would do it.

They headed back to the front of the house...making sure to grab a cookie or two on the way...and stepped outside. Shicksus then took out a second leather pouch. This one was filled with a shiny, silvery powder that he blew on the two boys. As before, they started to sneeze, stopped and then let out a tremendous, "AHHHHCHOOOOOO!" Then they were spinning and growing, and growing and spinning, until they were back to full height.

They ran straight into their own, much larger house, and quickly found their mother and father in the kitchen.

"Mom...Dad," Greg said, "We have something to tell you."

"What is it, guys," his parents asked.

"Well, every time you use the hose to give Buster a bath, I think a bunch of water leaks under the house. Will you look?"

"Sure," his father said, as he grabbed his toolkit and went outside. In just a few minutes, his father had found the problem and fixed the leak. Just like that, Shicksus' house was saved. Two small boys made a very big difference.

When Greg and Ben ran back to tell Shicksus what they had done they noticed that something had changed. They bent down to look at the place where the door had been, but it was gone. In its place was a small note. This is what it said:

Boys. I can't thank you enough. You've saved my house and I am forever grateful. If you ever need my help just send Buster to find me...he'll know where to look. In the meantime, I'll look after things for you and your family. Like I said, ... it's my job. Your friend, Shicksus.

Greg and Ben didn't see Shicksus again for many months and the next time they did see him it was quite an adventure.

On this particular day, Shicksus, was planning to go with Greg, Ben, and their family on their trip to the beach. As he is no bigger than Greg's hand, Shicksus decided that he would travel in Greg's beach duffel bag.

It was very cozy inside; overflowing with warm towels and even a large bed sheet Greg's parents use to lay out their picnics on the sand. Seeing that his traveling accommodations would prove to be very comfortable, Shicksus climbed into the bag and prepared for the long journey south...to the beach.

The next day, Greg and Ben ran out of the car and onto the beach. Their weeklong vacation had just begun and their heads were already filled with ideas about how they would spend the time.

First, Greg thought, *we'll need to build a giant sand castle. We'll have to do it quickly, before the tide comes in and washes the whole thing away.*

Ben, meanwhile, was thinking about playing in the water, rushing into the waves as fast as he can, and then riding the current back to the shore. *Bodysurfing*, he thought, *my favorite!*

Neither boy was aware of the little friend who had stowed away inside Greg's bag. Shicksus had no idea what he was going to do for a week at the beach. He only knew that he couldn't let his 'boys' travel this far without having him there to watch out for them.

The first few days were wonderful for everyone. Greg and Ben's parents were able to spend long days enjoying the sun as they lay out on the large sheet and beach towels. *A little sunburn seems a small price to pay for such a relaxing trip*, their father thought.

In the meantime, Greg and Ben busied themselves making tremendous sand castles, riding the waves, eating snow cones, and playing ball along the shore.

All the while, Shicksus kept out of sight. Since he was not needed, he took advantage of the fine weather himself by finding a sunny spot near the beach house. Although there were no tiny openings under the house for him to crawl into, he became perfectly content to sleep out under the stars...it was a nice change.

All was fine and relaxing...that is until their fourth day at the beach. It was that day that Greg and Ben's father realized that he had lost his ring...his wedding ring. He couldn't believe that it had simply slipped off his finger, but he had no idea where it could be. He simply never took it off...not even in the shower.

"How could this have happened," he cried. "I'm always so careful. Boys, have you seen my ring?"

The boys hadn't. They were so busy building their latest sand creation that they scarcely had time to remember to eat lunch, let alone pay attention to where their father might have put his ring.

"Perhaps I can help, boy!" a very familiar, gravely voice said near Greg's foot. "Shicksus?" Greg asked. "How did you get here?"

"I have my ways, boy, but we don't have time to talk about that now. If we're going to find your father's ring, we'd better get started." Both boys agreed and followed Shicksus towards the tiny camp he had made for himself near the beach house.

"Where did I put that thing," Shicksus muttered as he searched feverishly through his tiny things. "Ah ha! Found it."

"What did you find?" Ben asked.

Shicksus didn't answer, but held up a small leather pouch. It was very similar to the ones the boys had seen before, except that the powder it contained was a most unusual, mossy green.

"You're not going to make us small again...are you?" Greg asked, with a broad smile crossing his lips. "Not this time...I've got something better. Follow me."

The boys did as Shicksus asked and followed him farther down the beach. They soon came upon an odd looking hole in the sand. It looked as though it had been dug out by a very small shovel and then pounded flat.

"Are we going in there?" Ben asked.

"No, no, no," Shicksus laughed. "We came here to talk." With that, Shicksus began snapping his fingers very quickly and loudly.

The boys looked at each other, then at Shicksus and then down to the hole. At first it seemed that nothing would happen, and then suddenly there was movement down in the sand...in the hole. A large claw worked its way out and was followed by the biggest crab either boy had ever seen.

Shicksus appeared to be speaking to the crab, but neither boy could understand. It sounded like nothing but clicks and snaps to them. Seeing their puzzled faces Shicksus said, "Oh yes, I forgot the most important thing."

He withdrew a small pinch of the green powder and blew it on each of the boys; nothing happened, but the boys knew better than to think that would last. Suddenly they had the urge to sneeze. "Ahhh...ahhhhh...ahhhhhhhhh...." They sighed for a minute and then, "AHHHHHCHOOOOOOO!"

Greg and Ben just looked at each other for a long minute after that. They weren't spinning and shrinking and shrinking and spinning. In fact, nothing seemed to be happening at all, or so they thought.

"Hello boys...welcome to my beach," came a deep and somewhat raspy voice. When the boys turned, they realized that it was the crab that spoke.

Before they could ask how, Shicksus spoke up. "That's magic listening powder I sprinkled you with. It allows you to speak with all different sorts of creatures, but we have to hurry. The effects don't last long."

Shicksus then turned to the giant crab and said, "would you please repeat what you told me earlier."

"As I said, Shicksus, I think one of my crab brothers has found something that may belong to you. It's shiny and golden and round. Does that sound familiar?"

The boys became immediately excited and Greg shouted, "Yes, yes sir. That sounds like my father's ring. Where is it?"

"I think I can get it back for you, but will you do a favor for me first," the crab asked.

"Sure...anything," Ben replied.

"I couldn't help but notice those wonderful sand castles you and your brother have built. Would you please build me one over there?" The giant crab pointed his enormous claw a bit further up the shore. "I need a new house and I can't think of a pair of better architects.

With a sense of joy and determination, the boys set out to build the giant crab the best sand castle they had ever built. When it was done, the crab crawled in the front door and let out a whoop of laughter...the best a crab could manage anyway.

Within minutes, the crab had gathered his entire family to see what the boys had done. Greg noticed that the smallest of the crabs had a shiny golden, crown. As he looked more closely, he realized it was his father's ring.

"Where did you find it?" Greg asked the

young crab. "I'm sorry, I saw it come off and it was just so shiny I couldn't help myself," the small crab said. "I didn't mean any harm."

"I'm sure my father will be so happy to get this back that he'll forget all about how it was lost," Greg said. "Thanks for returning it."

"I hate to break up this teary moment, but we should get back...don't you think?" Shicksus asked. "Besides, in another minute you won't be able to understand each other anymore."

So Greg, Ben, and the crabs said their good-byes. Greg and Ben brought the ring back to their father and Greg was right. He was so happy to get it back that he didn't give a thought to asking the boys where they had found it.

As for Shicksus, he simply went back to the small camp he had set up for himself. He planned to enjoy a few more days in the sun. As it turned out he was wise to rest while he could, because the next time Greg and Ben needed his help it turned out to be an exhausting adventure.

However, that's a different story.

LEN SILVERMAN BIO

Len Silverman is a marketing professional with degrees from University of Florida and Emory Business School. He lives in Nashville Tennessee with his wife Tracey and his two boys, Greg and Ben. The boys were the inspiration for the story of Shicksus. As preschoolers, the boys came to require 'made up' bedtime stories. That made for a lot of fun and an environment ripe for the creation of some good tales. Shicksus quickly became a favorite story subject and many adventures were created, refined, and passed on through the nightly ritual.

Although the boys are now older, the ritual of story telling continues. Len hopes this creativity will become infectious and will help Greg and Ben through their school years and beyond.

Goat Talk
Julie Ryan Hannah

A woman and a man lived in a little cabin they had built themselves on the edge of a lovely green forest by a beautiful blue lake. They fished in the lake and foraged for berries and nuts in the forest. They also tended a small garden and kept a cow, a goat, and a few hens. It was altogether a very satisfactory life. The only thing they wished for was a little boat.

"We could have a fine time rowing on the lake in the evening," said the man to the woman.

"Yes, we could," she answered. "We are very lucky to live by this pretty lake."

One warm summer evening the man and woman sat outside on their little porch talking about the kind of boat they would like to have.

"I think the boat should be made of wood," said the man, "and have two sets of oars."

The goat, which had been nibbling the grass nearby, and listening to their conversation, ambled toward them. Putting his nose over the porch railing, the goat spoke to them, saying: "You should have a new cart instead of a boat."

You can imagine how surprised the man and the woman were when the goat spoke to them. Goats almost never do that, you know, and this goat was no different from any other goat in that respect. That is, until now. This conniving goat had been biding his time, waiting for the right moment to say what he had on his mind. *I am so smart,* he thought. *I am smarter than that man, and perhaps I am smarter than the woman, too. I should arrange things around here to suit myself.*

When the man had collected himself enough to reply to the goat, he asked: "What kind of new cart should we get?"

Right away that wily goat replied: "Well, your neighbors across the lake have a very nice one. It has a painted red side rail and steps down each side and red wheels with white spokes. It's quite handsome.

"We cannot afford a new cart," said the woman, who managed the family money. "You are right," said the man to the woman "What was I thinking?"

Not to be gotten rid of that easily, the goat spoke again. "I know how you can get extra money for a new cart," he said. "You can sell the cow. That cow is very troublesome. She has to be taken to pasture, she has to be fed and milked morning and night every single day."

"It would be a fine thing to be seen riding in a new cart," said the man, after a while.

"If we have any money to spend, we should get the little boat we have wanted for so long," said the woman. "Our old cart serves us very well." "You are right, of course," said the man. "What was I thinking?"

The man did not sleep well that night. The next morning, very early, the man and the goat had another conversation. Shortly after breakfast, although the woman protested loudly, the man hitched the old cart to the goat, and tied the cow to the cart.

"I'll return with the new cart before dark," said the goat. Off he went down the road, pulling the cart and cow behind him. The goat smiled to himself as he trotted along. *I will get rid of this detestable cow and this miserable cart at the same time. I am a genius.* The goat had long been jealous of the attention the couple paid to the cow. He had plotted to get rid of her at the first opportunity.

In the town square, the goat propped up the large COW FOR SALE sign the man had prepared. That brown-eyed beauty was soon sold and the money dropped into a small bag attached to the goat's harness. The goat immediately went down the street to the cart seller's shop and presented a note from the man saying he wished to buy a certain kind of very fine cart. The cart seller led the goat over to a yellow and white cart parked by the fence. *This is just what I had in mind,* thought the goat. He stood still and kept very quiet while the cart seller hitched him to the cart. In fact, he said not a word the whole time he was in town.

The money that was left after selling the cow and buying the cart belonged to the man and woman, of course, but the goat was still not satisfied. As he passed the hat maker's shop, he spied something in the window that made him stop and stare.

That hat would look wonderful on me. By my own wits I have this money, so I should spend it to please myself. But I must be clever about this.

That afternoon, after the chores were done, the man hitched the goat to the new cart, and he and the woman settled themselves inside for a ride. The goat took them around the lake and then into town. As he ambled slowly past the beautifully decorated window of the hat shop, the woman cried out: "Stop! I want to look at that hat." The man waited in the cart for what seemed a long time until, finally, the woman came out wearing a large green straw hat with a purple feather waving from the top.

"That is the most ridiculous hat I've ever seen," said the man. The woman, looking very upset, got in the cart and they headed for home.

I can't wait to try on that hat, thought the goat. He hummed a little tune to himself as he trotted along. The man and woman were silent as they rode in their handsome new cart. They did not seem to notice the beautiful trees that shaded the road, or the sun shining on the pretty lake.

The next morning, while the man was making some repairs to the porch, the goat stood near him

178

and said, "Wouldn't you like to go for a ride in the new cart?"

So, once again the goat was hitched to the cart and the woman and the man were seated inside. This time the goat turned onto the road going around the other side of the lake. Soon they came to a little white house with a weeping willow tree and a FOR SALE sign in the yard. The goat smiled as he strolled slowly past the house.

"What a pretty house!" the woman exclaimed.

"We should buy this house," said the man. "We cannot afford a house like this," said the woman. "You are right, of course," said the man. "What was I thinking?"

They decided to look inside anyway, and were amazed to see how bright and pretty the big rooms were. In no time at all the arrangements were made. They promised to pay a lot of money every month and moved into the new house. The goat made seven trips between the little cabin and the new house, the cart loaded with furniture and dishes and clothes. When he was finished, he returned alone to the little cabin by the lake.

After the goat left, the man and woman sat on the steps of the new house to rest. It was very quiet. "I miss the hens," said the woman, after a while. "Their soft clucking is such a happy sound. We will have to build a house for them."

"I miss my comfortable chair on the porch of our cabin."

When it began to get dark, they went inside to prepare their dinner. They could not find the wooden spoon or the iron stewpot and the stove would not work properly. They had to settle for cold bread and cabbage, and sat at the table eating their supper in tired silence.

The next morning the man and woman ate cold bologna sandwiches for breakfast.

"We have no eggs and no milk, because we have no hens and no cow," said the man. "And the stove doesn't work. Why did I ever listen to that goat? What could I have been thinking?"

"We all make mistakes," the woman replied.

"I'm starting to feel very foolish," said the man. "We must do something to put that goat in his place." "We need to get our happy life back," said the woman.

The man and woman walked to their little cabin. When they arrived they discovered the goat on the porch sitting in the man's favorite chair. He was wearing the woman's new hat and snacking on the straw doormat. He looked very surprised to see the man and the woman.

"What are you doing wearing my hat?" asked the woman. "And what are you doing sitting in my chair?" asked the man.

The goat said nothing. For once, he could think of nothing to say. The man and woman demanded twice more that the goat explain his behavior, but he remained silent.

Finally, the man said: "What are we doing, standing here demanding that a goat talk to us? Everyone knows goats do not talk. If anyone heard us, they would think we were both crazy."

Just then they heard a commotion, and turning, saw their beautiful cow loping into the yard, her bell clanging loudly from her collar. A sweating, gray-haired woman was in close pursuit.

"I'm sorry I bought this cow," said the gray-haired woman. "She's a terrible nuisance. She kicked the milk bucket over and this is the second time she has run away from me."

"Well," said the man slowly, "If you really feel that way, I guess I could give your money back and allow the cow to stay here."

"I would really like that," said the gray-haired woman.

"So would I," said the cow. The gray-haired woman gave the cow a startled look, but the man and the woman pretended they hadn't heard anything.

"I have been out in the sun too long," muttered the gray-haired woman as she walked away from the little cabin.

"And not another word from you!" said the man and woman to the cow as they led her back to a place in the shade "Or from you!" they said to the goat.

The next day, the man and woman put a sign on their new house. It read: HOUSE FOR SALE. The house was soon sold to a family with two children who were delighted with the willow tree. The new cart was returned to the cart seller in exchange for the old one. "I believe we have enough money for the little boat now," said the woman.

A few days later, as the couple sat on the porch, listening once more to the contented murmur of the hens, the woman said: "That hat looked better on that goat than it does on me. I think I'll take it back to the store." The man, who was not completely stupid, said nothing.

From that day forward, the goat knew he was better off to behave as other goats do. He never again spoke or tried to meddle in affairs that were none of his business. As for the man and the woman, they lived happily in the little cabin for the rest of their lives. And now and then they recalled that, once upon a time, they had made the mistake of listening to a goat talk.

JULIE HANNAH BIO

Julie Ryan Hannah lives on the Texas Gulf Coast with her beloved partner, Dave, and two cats, Skipper, the Siamese, and Hobbes, the tabby. Skipper cleans off her desk by shoving everything on the floor, while Hobbes unloads the printer and would like to answer the phone, but has such a drawl nobody can understand him.

The cats and how she came to have them have sometimes served as subjects for her writing. Julie writes short stories, has just completed a midgrade children's novel, and is active in her local writers group. Goat Talk is her third published story.

She likes to hike and kayak when she isn't writing, and is trying to get up the nerve to learn to sail.

Editorial Note: This story is set during the World War II era. *Rationing* is an unpleasant term likely to be unknown to young readers. There are moments, even in austere times, when the wishes of the heart must be followed.

Saturday Shoes
Connie J. Weber

There they were...behind the glass of the big display window, backed by a poster of Rita Hayworth advertising war bonds. Shiny wheels, long, gleaming white laces, pink pom-poms over the toes. "Are you sure?" Her friend Sharon's voice was a whisper.

"Mama said to buy something that I would wear. Something I would get a lot of use from." Meggie couldn't take her eyes off of them.

"Don't you think she was talking about *shoes*?"

Finally, Meggie tore her eyes away from the roller skates in Jamison's Hardware window. She turned to her friend. "But I'll wear these every Saturday. I bet I'll wear them more than I would any old church shoes!" She slid one hand into the

183

pocket of her jeans and fingered the book of ration coupons.

"I don't know, Meggie. What is your mom going to say? It's your last shoe coupon for this year. What if your feet grow? What if they shut down the roller rink?"

Both girls shivered at that last thought. But Meggie was determined. "How can my feet grow any more? They're already a size 10. And if they shut down the roller rink, I'll skate up and down Central Avenue. Let's go."

They went in through the huge double doors of the hardware store. Meggie had been inside one other time. Before her dad had left them, before the war, she had come in with him to buy a new faucet for the kitchen sink. She remembered that the cash register was over in the corner. They walked past nearly empty shelves that showed the effects of the war. So much was being rationed these days that the supply of tools, toasters, and towels was pretty sparse. A bulky man in striped overalls greeted them. Meggie noticed that the side buttons of his overalls were several inches away from the corresponding buttonholes.

"Good morning, ladies. How can I help ya this fine autumn day?"

Meggie put a hand to her short, light brown hair and twirled a lock of it around one finger. "I, um, well, I'd like to buy a pair of roller skates, please."

The man seemed to be sizing her up. "The price isn't bad, but I'd have to have a valid shoe coupon to go along with it." He sounded like he expected that to be the end of the conversation.

"Oh, yes. I know." Meggie pulled the coupon book out of her pocket.

Sharon was looking at the floor. Her hands were in the pockets of her faded jeans and she was shifting from one foot to the other.

The hardware man looked at Sharon and then back at Meggie. He hooked his thumbs around the straps of his overalls. "Like to roller skate, do ya?"

Meggie got the distinct feeling that he was stalling. "Yes, I do. I'm very good at it too. We skate every Saturday."

"And your mama gave ya the coupon book?" Definitely stalling.

"Yes." Meggie drew herself up to her full five feet, nine inches. "I wear a size ten, please."

Shaking his head, the man patted her shoulder. "The other two coupons for this year have expired by now. Ya don't want to waste your last shoe coupon on a pair of skates do ya?"

Meggie pulled back. "I don't believe that's any of your business. She was not going to be talked out of this by her best friend Sharon, let alone some old duffer at the hardware store.

"Alright then." He sighed. "They're $5.25 plus the coupon. All sales on roller skates are final." He looked at the girls out of the corner of his eye.

Meggie figured that he thought he'd drive them away with that last comment. But he was wrong. "I'd like to try them on now, please."

185

She held his gaze until he finally looked away. The large man shuffled behind the counter, muttering to himself. "Don't want no mamas down here this afternoon..." He disappeared into what looked to be a storeroom.

"Who does he think he is, my dad? I can buy roller skates if I want to. Boy! That makes me mad!" Sharon was still staring at her shoes. "What are you going to tell your mom, Meggie? You know she sent you out for shoes. And if you don't bring them back...I don't think you should do this."

Meggie was losing patience. Why was everybody trying to talk her out of this? She was fourteen years old and knew what she wanted. She had earned the money herself, for Pete's sake! What did anyone else care that she bought roller skates instead of boring old shoes? She *had* a pair of shoes. They had a few scratches and scuffs, but it wasn't anything that a little spit shine wouldn't cure. Her other pair of shoes had been ruined when the basement flooded, but these would last until they got more coupons. She'd make sure.

Ever since she'd learned to skate last winter, she'd longed for skates of her own. They used to spend every Saturday afternoon at the movies, but one week, Sharon's brother and his friend invited them to go along to the roller rink. For Meggie, a new world opened up. She finally found something she was good at, REALLY good. Within a few weeks, she had learned how to skate backwards. She was working on learning spins right now, and she needed a good pair of skates. The

186

two size tens for rent at the roller rink dug into the sides of her feet and left her with blisters. She was determined to have her own skates.

"Sharon, I'm a big girl. Mama might be mad, but this is *my* money and *my* ration coupon. This war will have to end someday. I'll get some new shoes then."

Sharon finally looked up and shook her head. "Your mom is going to hit the ceiling! She'll probably forbid you from going to the roller rink."

Meggie hadn't thought of that. It was true. Her mother had once stopped her from going to the movies for a whole month because she had stayed for the double feature without permission. But it hadn't lasted forever. She had to have these skates. And if Mama grounded her, she'd practice in the basement!

"Look, Sharon, I've waited my whole life to find something I'm good at." Meggie took Sharon's hand in hers. "When I'm on skates, I can forget about everything. I stop wondering where my dad is. I stop worrying about how much time Mama spends at work. I stop thinking about the war and the bombing and the Nazis. I feel free and happy and safe. I can't get all that from a dumb old pair of shoes."

Sharon didn't say anything. They heard the man in the storeroom moving boxes around. He was still talking to himself. Finally, he came through the door and returned to the counter.

Sharon squeezed Meggie's hand. Nothing more had to be said.

"I'm sorry, little lady. No size tens in the

back." The hardware man's apologetic look didn't hide the relief in his voice.

Meggie's heart sank. This was the only place in town that sold skates. She'd looked everywhere else. Even though it was the state capital, Cheyenne wasn't a very big place. "Are you sure? Maybe you missed them. Would you mind checking again?" Her voice was trembling.

His smile was just a little too sweet. "I checked twice. Real sorry, honey."

Sharon linked her arm in Meggie's. "Maybe they'll get some in another time."

"Not likely. Not a lot of call for roller skates these days." The man folded his arms and looked very satisfied with himself.

Meggie didn't know whether it was disappointment about the roller skates or her anger at the smug salesman, but tears were burning in her eyes. She shoved her hands into her pockets.

Sharon started to lead Meggie back toward the door. "Don't worry, Meg. Like you said, the war is bound to end someday. Then I'll bet there will be lots of size tens!" They walked out of the double doors and stopped at the window to look at the display once more.

It just wasn't fair! Her stupid old feet *would* have to be too big. It was hard enough to find blouses with the sleeve long enough, or slacks that made it down to her ankles, and now her big feet were stopping her from having the skates. The first tear slid down her cheek.

"Let's go down to the drug store. I'll buy us a Coke to split." Sharon dug through the pocket of her jeans. After a moment, she looked up at Meggie with a shattered expression. "Jeeze, Louise! Now I can't even find my nickel!" She threw her arm around Meggie's shoulders and squeezed.

The two lingered for another moment at the window before Sharon spoke again. "They are pretty, aren't they? Say..." Sharon craned her neck a little to get a better view. Then she stepped back and looked at Meggie's feet.

"What is it?" Meggie used the back of her hand to wipe at the tears that had made their way over her jaw and had started down her neck.

Sharon was smiling. "I could be wrong, but what size to you suppose those skates are?"

"Meggie's eyes widened. Do you think...?" Then she shook her head. "No. Probably not."

"You won't know if you don't ask." Sharon grabbed her hand and pulled her back through the doors. "Excuse me," she called out. "Sir? Could we take a look at those skates in the window?"

The man behind the counter looked up from the doughnut he was eating. "I thought you girls had gone." He didn't look pleased.

Now, Sharon was the assertive one. "Yes, sir, we had. You know, my friend has had her heart set on her own skates for a while. I was going to buy her a Coke, to console her, but I can't find the nickel I had a while ago. Anyway," she stepped right up to the counter and leaned in toward the man. "As we admired the skates in the window one last time before leaving, we got to wondering. Would you mind taking them out to check the size? My friend here would be very grateful."

One thing Meggie had always admired about her best friend was the way she could turn on poise and charm, like the flipping of a switch. Sharon cocked her pretty head to one side, looked up at the man with her big, blue eyes, and sent him the smile that Meggie had only seen Sharon's mother resist.

The man in the overalls seemed suddenly flustered. He looked at Meggie and then back at Sharon. Meggie watched his resolve crumble and his hard expression soften. "Well, I didn't realize it meant so darn much to ya, little lady. Let's just take a look, shall we?" He lumbered up to the front of the store and reached into the display.

Meggie could feel her heart beating, could hear it drumming in her ears. The man motioned for her to sit on the step that led to the display area, and then handed her the skates. She looked over at Sharon for a moment. Her friend gave her a wink of encouragement. Holding her breath, Meggie peeked inside the left skate, and saw a small "10" stamped along the heel.

It was hard to see through her tears, but Meggie managed to pull the laces loose and wiggle her foot inside. Sharon was frantically pulling at the laces of the right skate. With both skates in place and the laces tied, Meggie held onto Sharon's arm and pulled herself to standing. Now she was eye to eye with the hardware man. He had a smile on his face...a genuine one this time.

"They feel great!" Meggie whispered.

"Take 'em for a spin, little lady. I want to see how ya do." The man made a broad gesture with his arm toward the bare, wooden floor of the hardware store.

Meggie pushed away from Sharon and sailed toward the back of the store. It felt as though the skates were an extension of her feet. She whipped around and did a quick turn, and then rolled backwards toward Sharon and the hardware man.

"I think those skates were waiting for ya," the man said as Meggie sat down to pull the skates off and put her scuffed shoes back on.

They went back to the counter where Meggie produced the money and the ration book. The man tore the coupon out with great ceremony and then rang the price into the register. Meggie counted out the correct amount, and waited while the man put her new skates into a box.

Sharon was beaming. You know, your mom is going to have kittens."

Meggie couldn't let that thought cloud her mind right now. She was too excited to get to the rink to give the skates a real try.

The man handed her the box. "Has yer mama ever seen ya skate?" Meggie was startled by the question. "N...no, sir. Why""

He dropped the coins into the register one at a time. "Because I think if she saw how much ya love it, she might be more understanding." He cleared his throat and attempted to put a crusty expression back onto his face. "Just my opinion."

Meggie smiled as she took the box from the counter. "You might be right. Thank you." She and Sharon started toward the door.

"Ya forgot yer change." The man followed

them across the store. "But I gave you the exact change—five dollars and twenty-five cents. I didn't bring any more than that."

The man held out two shiny nickels, one in each hand. "Well, then, let's just say that we're running a special—each pair of skates sold today comes with two bottles of Coke." He put a nickel into the hand of each girl. "You ladies have a nice day, now."

CONNIE J. WEBER BIO

Connie Weber has been writing most of her life, and five years ago, she finally decided to let someone else read what she had written.

Saturday Shoes is her second story to be published, and was inspired by her mother's experiences as a young girl. Connie grew up in Wyoming and has lived in Oregon, Scotland, Utah, Connecticut, and Hawaii. She now lives in Bothell, Washington with her husband Warren, their eight-year-old son Coles, and an opinionated Springer Spaniel named Eli. She teaches special education to support her writing and love of travel.

Connie spends her time off reading, working in her garden, watching old movies, and cycling with her family. Aside from being published for the first time, her biggest accomplishment in the past year was learning how to snowboard (she's still working on how to get off the lift without falling...).

The Snow Queen's Carpet
Kelly Terwilliger

One gray morning a white rabbit hopped down the road thinking of lettuce. Quite by accident, he stumbled into a large black hat. Before he could hop out again a man picked up the hat and looked inside.

"A white rabbit!" he cried. "My lucky day! I have never been able to pull a rabbit from my hat, never! And now from nowhere a white rabbit appears!"

"Not from nowhere," interrupted the white rabbit. "I just left my house. I was on my way to get some lettuce from my garden over here."

"Details!" cried the man, who was a magician, but not a very good one. "The main thing is, now you can help me!" "I'm not sure..." began the rabbit.

"Pish posh!" interrupted the magician. "It will be perfect. For as long as I can remember, I have wanted to fly on the Snow Queen's carpet. Now, you can fetch it for me!"

"Why don't you fetch it yourself?" said the rabbit.

"Don't be silly!" said the magician. "I don't know how. I don't even know where the Snow Queen lives, but I do know how to send a rabbit there. It is the one spell I memorized during magician school," he added proudly.

"Wonderful," muttered the rabbit. "Who is this Snow Queen, anyway?" The magician didn't answer.

"All you have to do," he said, "is find the carpet and fly it back to my house. Here, I'll give you my address. Just make sure the Snow Queen doesn't notice you flying off. You know how people are when you take things without asking."

"Forget it!" said the rabbit. "I'm not going to steal a carpet!" But it was too late. The magician closed his eyes, waved his fingers, and muttered something like pingpongpuddleduddle. Then he disappeared. So did the rabbit.

A moment later the rabbit was sitting on the ledge outside a window of a high tower. He looked down with one eye and saw more towers and parapets and walls far below. A light snow was falling.

"You'd think he could at least send me to a door somewhere," said the rabbit. He peered at the

194

towers and walls beneath him. How was he ever going to get down?

Very carefully, so as not to lose his balance, he tapped a toenail against the windowpane. Nothing happened. Even if someone were inside, who would expect a visitor at this window? The rabbit felt cold and a little dizzy. He tapped again.

This time he heard a rustle--and a clank and a squeak as someone opened the inside shutters. An old man with a very long beard pressed his nose against the glass. He grinned and waved at the white rabbit and began to tug at the window. With a sudden jerk--so sudden the rabbit nearly toppled off the ledge--the window opened and the little old man grabbed the rabbit's ears just as he was about to fall.

"Goodness!" said the old man. "That was close, wasn't it? It's awfully nice of you to stop by. I don't get many visitors, you know!"

The rabbit glanced around. There was a narrow bed, a small bookshelf, and a chamber pot. The very tiny door appeared to be locked, and the old man had chains around his ankles.

As the white rabbit rubbed his ears, the old man sat down and began to fiddle with the chains. His beard kept getting in the way, but he chattered happily as he worked.

"Well then, shall we go down together? Now that you're here, we can, you see. When I came up here, oh what was it? A hundred years ago... to sulk, I told everyone I would not come down until a white rabbit appeared on the windowsill. They all said that would never happen, but I know if

195

you have the time and patience, anything will happen eventually!"

"Why would you want to sulk for so long?" asked the rabbit. The little old man shrugged.

"When you live forever, you can take some liberties," he said. At last he dropped the chains to the floor with a loud clatter. "Let's go!" he whispered. "We shall give the Queen a tremendous surprise!" He opened the tiny door, which was not locked after all, and he and the rabbit squeezed through.

They crept down a narrow stairway. It spiraled around and around and around. At the very bottom was another door.

"Shhh!" said the man. He pushed the door. It opened with an awful creak and the old man fell out into the room beyond. There, a beautiful woman sat at a large desk tapping her pencil and frowning. When the old man burst in, she gave him a glare. He scrambled up, hurried back behind the door, and closed it.

"Oops!" he said to the rabbit. "She hates to be disturbed when she's busy with affairs of snow." They waited in silence until they heard the queen's chair move and her footsteps, light as snowflakes, leave the room. Then they crept out.

"Follow me!" said the little man, "and keep to the shadows!" "Why?" asked the rabbit. "She knows we're here."

"Oh come now! It's just more fun this way!" said the little man. The rabbit sighed, and wondered how he would ever find a way home.

He hurried after the old man. They tiptoed down corridors, through hallways and arches, and up and down stairs, following the Snow Queen as quietly as they could and keeping out of sight. The white rabbit wished he could speak with the Queen--or anybody else for that matter but every time he tried, the old man snatched him back into the shadows with a chiding look. Finally, the queen went into a room and closed the door. The rabbit turned to the man.

"I've heard the Snow Queen has a flying carpet," he said. "Is this true?"

"Of course!" said the man, "and funny you should ask. She keeps it in that very room" he nodded at the closed door. "It's wonderfully soft," he added. "Quite like rabbit fur, come to think of it."

The rabbit didn't like this thought at all--no one really had rabbit-fur carpets, did they? "Does it truly fly?" he asked quickly.

"Of course," said the man. "And wherever it goes the snow falls." "How does it work?" asked the rabbit. "That I don't remember," said the man. "Can't be too hard. I suppose you need a password. Wait! Ready? Here she comes!"

Just then the Snow Queen opened the door and the old man gave a wild yodel and leaped in front of her, pulling the rabbit with him. A sheaf of papers the Queen had in her hands went flying into the air and floated down all around them. As the old man began to chortle gleefully, the white rabbit watched the papers scamper back into a pile with a whispering noise. The Queen picked them up.

"There you are!" she said. "I see you've finally decided to come down. Where did you find this rabbit?"

"Aren't you glad to see me?" asked the man eagerly. " Of course I am," said the queen. "But you hardly have time for sneaking around. You have one hundred years of work to catch up on, you know."

"Well, yes," mumbled the man. "I name the snowflakes," he explained to the rabbit. "One hundred years of anonymous snowfalls. Can you imagine? Now I have to remember all those snowflakes and all their names! Which I do, of course," he added defensively. "Perfect names and every one of them different. Whippsichord, Frothediddle, Joshualee! Mintith, Plenteth, and Allabunch!" He began to chant.

"Well then," said the queen. "Off with you. And what about the rabbit?" "I let him in at the window upstairs," said the man as he skipped down the hall.

"I was sent by a magician," said the rabbit nervously, wondering if the carpet really was made of rabbit fur. "He … he wanted me to steal your flying carpet. But I just want to go home. I was on my way to get some lettuce and I still haven't had any breakfast."

The queen looked at him sharply and the rabbit squirmed beneath his white fur. "I haven't had lettuce in a long time," she said at last. "It doesn't grow well in snow. I will fly you home if you will get me a bunch or two."

"Of course, your majesty," said the white rabbit, bowing. He felt faint with relief.

"Do you have the address of the magician?" the Snow Queen went on. "Yes," said the rabbit. "And ... I have a question, your highness."

"What is it?"

"What is your carpet made of?" The rabbit braced himself for the reply. The Snow Queen smiled.

"The down of clouds," she said.

That very afternoon the white rabbit flew on the Snow Queen's carpet. He learned the password, but I won't say it here in case that magician ever reads this. It was a flight so soft and silent, trailing snowflakes as it went, that the rabbit wished it might never end.

"That is the danger of such a carpet," said the Queen. "I occasionally lose track of time myself, and then we end up with terrible blizzards." She brought the carpet down beside the rabbit's house.

The rabbit hopped to the ground. "I'll be right back," he said and hurried off to his garden to fetch two heads of lettuce.

When he returned the Snow Queen was gone. Only a damp patch remained where the snow carpet had rested. On his door was a note.

Sorry. Had to leave in a rush. Will be back some day for lettuce.
Yours Truly.
The Snow Queen.

So the rabbit sat down and ate both heads of lettuce himself. They were very good.

The magician meanwhile got his own note, along with an enormous pile of snow on top of his house, which took forever to melt.

Come to the castle yourself and ask nicely. I might give you a ride. Meanwhile, find something better to do than harass rabbits into stealing what isn't theirs or yours.
The Snow Queen.

The magician never made it to her castle. He didn't know how. However, he framed her note and hung it in his living room and behaved much better after that.

Editorial Note: Stories for *Beyond Time and Place* were numbered for blind judging so it came as a surprise that four authors had each written two winning stories.

For KELLY TERWILLIGER BIO, see next story

The Cricket And The Stone Fairy
Kelly Terwilliger

One day as he was walking home, Peter kicked a pebble. "Ouch!" said a voice. Peter picked up the little stone. He inspected it closely, but it looked like an ordinary pebble. He put it in his pocket.

"Ouch!" Peter looked again and there at his feet was a cricket clutching a tiny violin case.

"I'm sorry," said Peter. "Are you hurt?"

"It's a wonder my leg didn't snap right off the way you kicked," said the cricket. "You must take me to the cave where the Stone Fairy lives. She will fix me. I will ride on your shoulder."

Peter was surprised, but he picked up the cricket and the violin and put them on his shoulder. "Careful!" cried the cricket. "I am very delicate!"

"Where is the Stone Fairy's cave?" asked Peter, when the cricket had settled down. "Over the hills and far away," said the cricket with a yawn.

Peter hoped the cave wasn't too far away. Just in case, he stopped to leave a note for his mother and packed a little knapsack with crackers and cheese and a pair of warm socks.

Then Peter walked. He walked for a long time and the road spooled out behind him like a silver thread.

After a while the ground grew soft underfoot. The air felt damp and smelled of wild azaleas, and clouds settled in white puffs among the trees. They had reached the hills. Peter began to climb. He'd heard rumors of blue dragons in these hills. Now and then he glanced over his shoulder, but the path was quiet.

"It's terribly damp," complained the cricket suddenly. "I need a poultice... and soup! I need a little blanket."

Peter did not know what a poultice was, and he did not have any soup.

"Would you like some crackers and cheese?" he asked, but the cricket declared he did not like crackers and cheese. Peter felt in his pocket for a handkerchief. He found the pebble and a little piece of red felt. He pulled out the felt and wrapped it around the cricket.

"I wonder where we go from here," Peter said. Something moved in the trees to his left and Peter spotted a unicorn grazing on a patch of sorrel.

"Excuse me!" he called, but the unicorn instantly disappeared. "They are never much use," said the cricket, yawning.

Up ahead they came to a signpost. "TRA LA LA" read Peter. "Well, that's not very helpful."

"OH WELL" read the next signpost.

Peter shook his head. "Peculiar place, these hills."

"Are you sure they are the right ones?" asked the cricket.

"I don't know!" said Peter. "I've never been to this cave. I've never even heard of it."

"Well, my goodness, you're the one leading the expedition," said the cricket. "I'm counting on you, you know."

Peter wondered if all crickets were so difficult. It started to rain, so he carefully put the little fellow into his knapsack.

"In a knapsack indeed! " muttered the cricket from inside the pack. "Am I baggage? Is that what I am?"

Peter kept walking. At last the path became so wet he ducked beneath some trees. He huddled against a large blue rock, scaly with lichen. Suddenly the rock shifted and gave a loud snort. With a gasp, Peter jumped aside. An enormous blue dragon lay curled between the trees, fast asleep.

"What is it? What is it?" cried the cricket from inside the knapsack. "Let me see!" He poked his head out of the bag. "A dragon!" crowed the cricket. "Hurray! Let's play a trick!"

"No!" said Peter, but the cricket was already crawling out of the knapsack.

"I thought your leg was hurt," said Peter.

"It is! It is! Oh! The pain!" But the cricket hopped to the ground with his good leg and began to gather up handfuls of pine needles.

"What are you doing?" said Peter.

"Watch this!" cried the cricket, and he poked a little bunch into the dragon's nostril. Peter watched, horrified. The dragon snorted, coughed, and then sneezed a shower of flames and sparks, starting a small fire.

"A fire!" cried Peter. "We must put it out before it spreads!"

"Don't worry," said the cricket placidly. "It's so damp here, it will go out in a moment." Which in fact it did.

"See?" said the cricket, but Peter was already putting him back into the knapsack, not so gently this time, and hurrying away from the sleeping dragon.

The rain thinned to a faint drizzle, and then faded away altogether. They reached the top of the hills. Peter spotted another signpost ahead.

"EVERYWHICHWAY" it read, and beside it, another sign announced "SOMETIMES IT'S ALL VERY FAR AWAY".

Peter decided to stop and have some cheese.

"Why are you stopping now?" asked the cricket. "Surely it's not time for lunch already! My leg hurts."

Peter looked at him. "I'm hungry and I'm going to eat the rest of my cheese which you don't like anyway, and if you are in such a hurry, you can tell me where we go from here, because I certainly don't know."

The cricket sighed a very small cricket sigh. "I don't know either," he said. "Stone fairies are the protectors of crickets, and there ought to be one around here somewhere." He was silent for a moment. "Please don't leave me here."

"I wouldn't do that!" said Peter. He finished his cheese and picked up the cricket once more.

Down they went, to the right, to the left, and around a boulder. From a large outcropping of rock two trees hung nearly upside down, and curled up again at the tips. Beneath them was a tiny cave. "Do you suppose we should try it?" asked Peter.

"Oh yes!" said the cricket. "Of course, it might be a dragon's lair in hills like these--why did you have to choose hills with dragons anyway?" Peter sighed. Then he took a deep breath and ducked into the cave.

It was dark and musty. Peter thought it was much more likely to harbor a dragon than a fairy. As his eyes adjusted, he could see light sifting down from far above. The ceiling of the cave was very high. Peter wondered what to do next. He was about to ask the cricket, when a faint voice called, "You're here!"

Peter looked up and saw a very old, very tiny lady with faded wings the colors of pale stone. She was sitting on a ledge of rock.

"Are you the Stone Fairy?" Peter asked.

"I am," she said. Her hands were gnarled and her face was covered with tiny wrinkles. She was beautiful. "I have lived alone here for a thousand years. At last you have brought my friend!"

"Your friend?" said Peter.

"I don't think we've ever met," interrupted the cricket. "I just came to get a leg fixed up, if you do that sort of thing. I hope you do."

"You are not the friend I meant," said the fairy kindly, "but of course I will fix your leg. I am a protector of crickets, after all." She floated down and placed her tiny dry hands upon the cricket. "There," she said after a moment. "As good as new."

"Now!" The fairy smiled and turned to Peter. "The friend I mean is in your pocket." Peter was puzzled. Had someone crawled into his pocket? He reached in very cautiously. He felt pine needles, cracker crumbs, and the pebble. He brought out the pebble. "This is all I have," he said. "I'm afraid if anyone did crawl in, he or she crawled out again. I'm sorry."

The fairy was not listening. She took the pebble in her thin little arms. She held it for a long time, and then she set the pebble down. Peter heard a cough. The next thing he knew the stone began to uncurl. A head lifted, arms unwrapped, knees unfolded.

Where the stone had been a fairy now sat. This one too looked very, very old with pale, translucent wings. It blinked at Peter, then at the cricket. At last, it saw the Stone Fairy.

The two fairies looked at each other. Then they reached out their dry and ancient hands. The cricket began to play a tune so beautiful that Peter nearly started to cry.

"There, there," said the cricket. "No need to cry, though my music is exquisite, isn't it? Bringing two old friends together again. You must be pleased!"

Peter didn't know what to say.

"I would love to give you a gift," said the Stone Fairy at last, still holding her companion's hand, "but I don't have anything except rocks and dust... and this cave. Would you like this cave?"

"I don't think so," said Peter. "I prefer blackberry patches and little streams, but thank you for the offer. You are very kind."

"So are you, my dear!" said the fairy. "May you find a friend as wonderful as mine!" Then the two fairies flew together up and out of the cave. "Goodbye!" they called. "Goodbye!"

"Wait!" cried Peter. "Where are you going?" But the fairies were already too far away to hear him.

The cricket finished the last notes of a quiet tune. "Well I feel much better," he said. "Thank you for bringing me all this way. Will you take me home with you?"

"I don't know the way home," said Peter.

"You don't know the way? Well, I don't know the way here, but crickets always know the way home!"

And with his two good legs, the cricket led them back down the hills and all the way home, playing his violin as they went.

KELLY TERWILLIGER BIO

Kelly Terwilliger, along with her husband, Leo, and two sons, Jacob and Eli, lives in the woods on the side of a hill in Eugene, Oregon. They share their home with a flock of chickens, some crotchety guinea pigs, a fire-bellied toad, and a small black hamster named Fred. Needless to say, there's plenty of inspiration in this menagerie.

These two stories each grew out of a handful of words: *rabbit, hat,* and *snow* in one case, and *cricket* and *fairy* in the other. "It's a game I play sometimes--I carry a few words around and see what sort of story coalesces. I'm usually surprised."

She has had a story published in Spider Magazine. Kelly is also a poet and an artist, and works as a storyteller-in-residence at local schools.

WE WISH YOU
ADVENTURE AND JOY ON
YOUR JOURNEY THROUGH
TIME AND PLACE.....

Notes and Ordering Information

The author of the First Place Winning *Twilight Among Cheese Clouds* donated his prize money to the Reach Out and Read literacy program.

That was the impetus for the **Beyond Time and Place Project** to focus on reading programs, classrooms, and libraries.

During the editing process, we passed along some of the stories to instructors teaching English as a second language to adults. They reported that the stories were suitable to their work and enjoyed by their students.

Linden Hill Publishing plans to continue its work with literacy programs.

To contact any of the contributing authors, visit www.lindenhill.net or email lindenhill@lindenhill.net. Individual authors and the publishers are available for speaking engagements and writing workshops.

TO ORDER *Beyond Time and Place*
- Online at www.lindenhill.net
- By Mail:
  Send $15 single copy + $2.50 S&H
  [MD residents add 5 % sales tax] in US funds to:

Linden Hill Publishing
11923 Somerset Avenue
Princess Anne, MD 21853

For multiple copy rates, please contact
Linden Hill Publishing

Linden Hill Publishing also has a wide selection of other books available that can be ordered online on our secure server. Learn more about these books on the website.